Now You Wanna
Come Back 2

Now You Wanna
Come Back 2

Anna Black

www.urbanbooks.net

Urban Books, LLC
300 Farmingdale Road, NY-Route 109
Farmingdale, NY 11735

Now You Wanna Come Back 2

ISBN 13: 978-1-64556-245-0
ISBN 10: 1-64556-245-X

First Mass Market Printing September 2021
First Trade Paperback Printing October 2020
Printed in the United States of America

10 9 8 7 6 5 4 3 2 1

Distributed by Kensington Publishing Corp.
Submit Orders to:
Customer Service
400 Hahn Road
Westminster, MD 21157-4627
Phone: 1-800-733-3000
Fax: 1-800-659-2436

Now You Wanna Come Back 2

Anna Black

Chapter One

Leila held her stomach as she glared out the window of her empty store. She was pregnant with baby number three and wondering how she could be losing her store in the middle of what was supposed to be the best time of her life. Rayshon had a booming business and was opening his third location, but eBooks had been the downfall to her store's success. After four years of so-called making it through the depression, recession, or whatever society was calling folks having no money nowadays, she wondered how electronic books had grown so fast.

"Damn, won't they miss the smell of the pages? Now, people have to plug in their books. Ain't that some shit?" she said, shaking her head. She thought about the Kindle Rayshon had gotten her for her birthday that year. It was still in its box. "What would really piss me off is to get to the climax of my book, then my battery dies, and there's no place to plug in. I would wanna punch somebody, that's for damn sure." She watched the shippers load the last boxes of her books onto the truck. "Damn damn damn. This is all I ever wanted, and now I have to wait for online orders. Shit."

She walked over to the counter and picked up her phone. She knew Rayshon wasn't available, but she called him anyway. "Hey, babe, it's me. I just wanted to tell you that I'll meet you at the house for dinner. I do hope that you can make it this time. My day has been hell, and your daughter has kicked a few field goals in my belly, and I don't want to put RJ to bed alone tonight," she said and hung up.

She looked around. Her eyes burned with tears, but she blinked them back. *All is not lost,* she told herself. *My online bookstore has got to bring in some profit.*

She did a quick walk-through of her now-empty space. It was still hers until it sold, and she prayed that it wouldn't take forever. She had no other use for it, and she was fresh out of ideas.

"We're headed to the storage, Mrs. Johnson," the driver said.

Leila nodded. "Okay, Chad. You know that everything is labeled. Please inform your workers to place the boxes in their appropriate spaces that are labeled in my storage. As you can see, I'm not in any shape to be moving boxes around." She held her tummy. She was a week away from being eight months, and the little girl in her womb was a kicker.

"No worries, Mrs. Johnson. We'll take care of everything. By the way, I am sorry to see your store closing. My wife only comes to your store for her books, and she is torn up too."

Leila was touched. "Thanks, Chad. Let her know that she can still order on my website. Leila's Books will still be available online until I'm sold out," she said with a smile. Behind her smile was a frown, but she didn't want to show any emotion.

"Will do, Mrs. Johnson," Chad said.

After he left, Leila looked around and wondered if she should try something else with the space. Maybe a daycare, since she was having another baby or an internet café, she wondered and quickly dismissed the daycare idea. She could do a café because she could tolerate adults, but she had no interest in putting up with strangers' children.

She grabbed her purse and keys and took one last look before she turned out the lights. Then she locked the door and headed to her truck. She drove a few blocks down to Rayshon's gym and hoped that he was there. He had just opened a new location, and she was glad that folks cared enough about their bodies to make him a successful business owner since no one cared about reading books with real pages anymore.

While her business declined, her husband's business was on an incline. In four years, his business had sky-rocketed while hers sank deeper and deeper into the ground. Leila congratulated Rayshon, but deep down, she didn't like that she was going nowhere, and he was pulling business in like a magnet. There had been days when she didn't even have to open because she'd get only one or two customers, and the first question they would ask after confirming the book was in stock was, "Is it available on Kindle?" Kindle had become a name that Leila despised, and she had wanted to punch Rayshon in the throat when he had given her one.

"No more featured authors, no more visits with the famous authors that had a line around the corner, and no more book release parties. God, I'm going to miss my store," she said to herself as she parked in the employee's parking area. She was sad not to see her husband's Denali, but she parked anyway, just to go inside to check on things.

She walked past the front desk and gave a few brief hellos and made her way back to what used to be

Rayshon's main office. His new manager, Ankwan, was on the phone, smiling like he was engaged in a call that was *not* business related.

"Hey, look, babe, I'll hit you back," he said and quickly hung up the phone. "Leila, what brings you by?" He sounded like he wasn't too happy to see her.

"Do I need a reason?" she asked and put her purse on the desk.

"Naw, I was just wondering. Ray hasn't been by here in days, and you popping in is like . . . rare."

"Well, as you know, my store closed today, and since I'm less than a mile away, I decided to drop in," she said, rubbing her belly. It was sore from the abuse that was going on from Kung-Fu-master-get-me-the-hell-up-outta-here-baby-number-three.

"Yeah, I heard, and I'm sorry. Ray told me in our last staff meeting."

"Oh, okay," she said with a fake smile. "I was just in the neighborhood, you know, and I thought maybe Ray would be at this location, but I see he's not," she said, grabbing her purse. "I'll let you get back to business," she told him and turned to walk out, and Ankwan didn't stop her. She knew he was anxious to call back whomever he was talking to earlier.

Leila got into her truck and called Ray again. Voicemail answered once more. She hung up without leaving a message and called Devon.

He answered on the second ring. "Hey, Lei."

"Hey, Devon, it's me, Lei," she said.

"I know. I just answered and said, 'Hey, Lei.'" He laughed lightly. "What's up?"

"Ummm . . . I know this is last minute, but since this is your weekend with DJ, do you think you can keep RJ tonight too? I had a tough day with the store closing, and I need a mommy break."

"Sure, that's not a problem, but you know how Ray gets when RJ stays with me overnight."

"I know, Devon, but Ray keeps these long hours now. With the third gym opening, he's hardly home to help me, and my stomach is *so* sore. I just can't do it tonight. By the time Ray gets home, he won't even realize that they're both gone."

"Okay, Lei, no worries. And I'm sorry about the store, sweetheart. I know how much that place meant to you. And so what if Ray is opening his third gym? He should be at home helping you. I know this pregnancy is hard for you, and I wish I could be there to help you."

"Come on, Devon. Don't, okay? Ray is a good man and a good husband and a great dad. He's just been swamped. So, don't."

"I know, Lei, and I didn't mean anything by it. I am not trying to upset you. I'll get the kids and give you a break. What time will you guys be home?"

"In an hour or so. Deja is already home with Tab, and as soon as I get off with you, I'm going to call her to get their overnight bags packed. I'm on my way to pick up li'l Ray now." She paused. "Are you sure, Devon? I'm not interfering with any of your plans with Deja, am I?"

"Lei, it's my weekend to get DJ, so I have no plans with her tonight. But tomorrow, you must get RJ by five, because Deja and I have a date."

"No problem, Mr. Vampelt. I wouldn't dare ruin my daughter's date," she said with a smile.

She and Devon were like best friends now, and he was the best father on the planet when it came to Deja. Even though she and Rayshon did well financially, Devon paid child support to the max and still did all the extras without complaint.

"Okay, well, I'll see you in an hour. Make sure you pack DJ's swimsuit because she's going to need it," he said.

Leila chuckled. "Okay, I will, Devon, but you know I need you to keep an eye on her in the water. She thinks she's Flipper and tries to dive in the deep end." She pulled into the daycare parking lot.

"Lei, I got this."

"I know, babe," she said and caught herself. "I mean, Devon. I know," she said and hit the *end* button.

She went inside and picked up her son, and then she headed home.

"Hey, Mrs. J—Deja has eaten, and Li'l Ray's dinner is in the warmer. I cleaned everything in the kitchen, and the kids' bags for their sleepover with Mr. Vampelt are by the door."

"Wow, thanks, Tabitha, but one last thing. I'm going to need you to grab Deja's swimsuit, please. I forgot to tell you to pack it."

Tabitha dashed toward Deja's room. Leila knew she had something going on or somewhere to be because she was short in conversation and exited the room too quickly.

"Hey, DJ," she said. "Your dad will be here shortly to pick you guys up."

"You guys? I thought it was only going to be my daddy and me this weekend?"

"Well, RJ is gonna tag along for one night to give Mommy a li'l me-time."

Deja frowned. "Why can't Daddy Ray keep RJ for your me-time?"

Leila was about to answer, but Tabitha walked back into the kitchen.

"Deja's swimsuit is all packed. Is there anything else, Mrs. Johnson?"

"Umm, no, Tab. We're good. Enjoy your weekend," Leila said.

Tabitha kissed the kids goodbye and promptly exited. Devon arrived not too long after, and finally, Leila was all alone. She looked to see what Tabitha cooked and turned up her nose at the ground beef and pasta cheese dish that was in the pot. She grabbed a bowl to refrigerate it, then washed the pot and put it away before walking upstairs.

At the top, she sighed. The beautiful three-level home that she and Rayshon had purchased was so lonely lately because he was never home. She took a shower and sat in her baby's nursery.

"Things are supposed to be better, Ray. You promised me that things would be great, but they are not," she said aloud, rubbing her belly. "How did we create this distance? No, how did *you* create this distance?"

She dozed in her rocker, thinking that things were perfect until work came before their marriage. Ray had been her comfort, but now she had to comfort herself.

The countdown to the closing day of her store had approached quickly, and every day, Rayshon treated it as if it were no big deal. "Lei, baby, don't worry," was all he'd say. "This will give you more time with the kids and time to enjoy your pregnancy."

She couldn't believe that he took it so lightly. Her dream was now a nightmare, and she was starting to feel like she was all alone in her marriage.

Chapter Two

"I think I need to see something a little bigger," Ray told Kennedy and watched her put the two-carat diamond pendant back. "My wife has had a terrible week, and I want to put a smile on her face for a change."

"I see," Kennedy said. "I know exactly what would make a woman feel better. May I show you something else?"

"Sure. I just want to cheer her up." He followed Kennedy over to several cases from where they were.

"Now this," she said, showing him a diamond tennis bracelet that looked amazing under the store's fluorescent lights, "would *definitely* put a smile on *my* face if I were having a bad week."

"Yes, it's beautiful, but I don't know," he said. Leila had a tennis bracelet similar to that one already. "You're the owner of this store, aren't you?"

"Yes, I am," Kennedy said. She smiled with pride. "I am the first female descendant to get my own store," she shared.

"Really? That's great, Kennedy, congrats," Ray offered.

"Thank you," she said with the same bright smile graced on her face. "So, tell me, what are you looking for today?"

"Show me something that would help to ease your pain if this store went outta business, and you needed to be cheered up," he said.

Kennedy showed him another case and then called for her assistant from the break room, and she was out front in a flash. "Teresa, please get Mr. Johnson a glass of champagne while we find a gift suitable enough to cheer up his wife." She turned back to Rayshon. "Now, this is what we call our High Rollers Case. Anything from this case would make the saddest person happy."

"Well, let's see what you got." Rayshon reached for the glass of champagne the young lady handed him and took a sip. "Wow, this is good."

"Thank you. We just recently added a refreshment station, and customers now come in just for a drink and a snack." Kennedy laughed lightly as she unlocked the case. She reached in and grabbed a pair of earrings. "Okay, these earrings are one of our popular items," she said and went on to give Rayshon more details about them. After she showed him some more items, he asked to see a diamond necklace. Kennedy smiled. "Oh, wow, this is one of my favorite pieces. This would certainly make a woman not only feel better but want to reward you." She winked.

Rayshon admired it. "This *is* lovely. I know Leila will love it."

"Leila . . . Leila. I know Leila is sorta a common name, but I know a Leila who just went out of business. Your wife isn't from Leila's Books, is she?" Kennedy asked.

Rayshon was surprised she knew of his wife's store. "Yes, today was the last day of business for her."

"Oh, Mr. Johnson, I'm *so* sorry. I've been going to her store for several years. My husband has a restaurant, not even a block down from her store."

"Wow, small world. The owner of the restaurant—your husband, Julian, of course—is a member at my fitness center down the street."

"Shut up! *You're* Mr. Johnson of Johnson's Physicals?"

"Yes, I am."

"I heard you just opened your third location," she said.

Ray sipped his drink again. "Yes, while my business is growing through the roof, my wife's barely held on this year," he said sadly.

"Wow, tell Leila that I am deeply sorry. This place is my baby, and even though we have some restaurants and nightclubs, I still love this store, so I can imagine how she feels."

"I know. That is exactly why you have to gift wrap this lovely necklace for me, so I can try to cheer her up. Opening my third location has had me swamped, and I work so many hours now. I know my wife thinks I'm the worst guy on the planet, but I'm not. I honestly hate that she had to give up the store, and it kills me that I am having so much success. I can't even look at her. I don't know what to say to make her feel better. She's pregnant with our third child, and I don't want her stressing, so to keep my sanity, I work. I move around."

"Well, Mr. Johnson, I can't tell you how to handle your marriage, but I will tell you that working and avoiding her isn't going to make her feel better. Even if you simply hold her hand, just show her that you wanna be there for her."

He nodded in agreement. "Yeah." He was used to being able to cheer Leila up, but with this one, it was hard because she made him feel bad at times for his business being such a success.

"You finish your champagne, and I'll have this wrapped right away for you," she said and moved to the back to have it gift wrapped.

Rayshon left the jewelry store and headed to the flower shop. He looked down at his phone and saw he had missed a few calls from Leila, so he listened to her voicemails, and it was all the same about him not being home for dinner, and she needed him to do this or that. He knew her words were true, but he wasn't away doing leisure shit. He was working, but that night he was anxious to get home. He hadn't had dinner with his family in weeks.

When he walked in, he was surprised that the house was so quiet. He went into the kitchen and was a little disappointed because there were no pots on the stove, and he didn't see any takeout. He put his briefcase on the kitchen island and removed the KBanks Jewelers bag, then took it and the flowers and walked upstairs to find her. He went into the master bedroom first, but there was no sign of her. Then he stuck his head into his son's room, thinking she'd be there with RJ, but she wasn't there either. He knew Deja should have been with Devon, but he looked in her room anyway. Leila wasn't there either. Her truck was in the garage, so he wondered where they were.

He stood in the hall and noticed a light coming from the baby's room and knew that's where she was. He gently pushed the door open to find Leila sleeping peacefully in her rocker. He approached slowly to keep from scaring her and leaned in and kissed her forehead. She opened her eyes, and he smiled.

"Ray, when did you get home?" she asked.

"A couple of moments ago. How are you feeling? Where's RJ?" he asked.

She rubbed her face. "Umm, RJ went to Devon's with Deja."

"Where did he take them?"

"Home. I wasn't feeling well, so Devon agreed to take him overnight for me to get some rest. Please don't make a big deal of it, okay? I know you don't like RJ staying the night."

"So why did you allow him to go overnight?" he asked.

Leila could hear the irritation in his tone. "Because you have been working every weekend and staying out past his bedtime a lot lately, and I needed a physical and mental break from him, Rayshon." She got up from the rocker.

Ray changed his tone. "Listen, it's fine, okay?" He wanted to cheer her up and not make her upset. "And these are for you," he said, handing her the flowers. He kissed her. "And this is also for you," he said, giving her the gift.

"What's this?" she asked, setting the flowers on the baby's changing table.

"This is a little something to say that I love you, and I'm proud of you, and I'm sorry your store closed," he said.

Leila's eyes welled up with tears. She slowly opened the pretty package and gasped when she saw the beautiful necklace. "Oh, Ray. Baby, this is lovely. This is beautiful, baby." She smiled, admiring it.

"You like it?" he asked, happy that she was delighted.

"Like it? I *love* it, but I have to pee," she said and handed him the box. She hurried down the hall, and he grabbed the flowers and followed her.

"I'm gonna head downstairs," he said. He went down to the kitchen and grabbed a vase for the flowers.

She joined him within minutes. "The necklace is beautiful, babe. Thank you," she said.

He walked over to her and embraced her. "I'm glad you like it. And the saleswoman knows you. Her name is Kennedy Roberson."

"Yes, I know her. She was one of my loyal customers. Her husband owns the restaurant on the corner."

"Yes, Julian. He's also a member of the gym."

"I know. She told me back when she was pregnant with her twins. She swore she'd join too after she had the babies, but I guess things change."

"Yep, baby, sometimes they do," he said and moved over to the wine cooler.

"God, I wish I could have that right now," Leila said. Her eyes watered.

"You can, babe. You know one glass won't hurt."

"I know, but the way I feel, I want to have an entire bottle," she said, wiping her tears.

"Aw, come on, Lei. We have talked about this, babe, and talked about it. It's not the end of the world."

"It's easy for you to say, Rayshon, because your dream of owning a gym has come true. And not only do you own one, but you also own *three,* and my one and only bookstore is closed." She pouted, leaned back against the counter, and put a hand on her stomach. "This little girl is abusing this one spot right here, and I just want to scream," she sobbed and made a frowning face.

Ray rushed over to her side. "Come on, Leila, baby. Why are you getting upset about this all over again? Come on, baby, and sit down. You're getting worked up, and you know it's not good for you or the baby." He led her into the family room. She sat on the couch, and he sat in front of her on the coffee table. "I keep telling you that I'll take care of us. You can be a full-time mom to our children and relax and take care of us now, without Tabitha."

"Ray, please . . . Don't give me that same old what-I-can-do-now. Are you not hearing me? I loved my store. I loved being around my books and getting up every day, servicing customers in my store. That meant so much to me, Ray, and I don't have that anymore. I loved having authors visit and read from their novels and having release parties, and now, all that is gone."

"What do I mean to you? What do the kids mean to you?" he asked.

Leila stood up. "Ray, thank you for the flowers and the necklace," she said, walking away.

"Where are you going?" he yelled behind her.

"To Christa's," she said, slipping her swollen feet into her flip-flops.

"Why? I came home early to be with you and to make you feel better, Leila, not for you to run out on our conversation."

"You know what, Ray? I never thought there would come a day in this marriage that you would not understand me," she said, moving swiftly.

"What? What are you talking about? You're acting as if the world has come to an end because your bookstore closed, Leila, when you have so many other things to be grateful for."

She nodded at him after snatching her keys from the counter near the garage door. "I know what I have, and I am grateful, but what you fail to realize, Mr. Johnson, is that bookstore was a part of my life. Not more important than you and the kids, but just as important—and I lost it. If I cry too much or bother you with my loss, I'm sorry," she yelled and walked out the door, slamming it.

Ray banged his fist on the island, wondering how this had turned into such a horrible night when he was only trying to make things right.

Chapter Three

"Hold on, Devon," Christa said, getting up from the sofa. "Someone's at the door," she said and walked over to the peephole. "It's Leila. Let me call you back," she said and ended the call. She opened the door and could tell her friend had been crying. "Leila, what's wrong? Come in," she said and shut the door.

"I need to talk, but first the bathroom," Leila said.

Christa nodded. Over the years, she and Leila had grown close, and now that she and Devon were seeing each other, they saw each other even more. Christa went into the kitchen and grabbed some bottles of water from the fridge and sat on the sofa as she waited for Leila to return.

"I'm sorry to come by so late, but Devon has the kids, and I'm trying to get away from them right now. I don't need my kids to see me cry another day, you know?" she said with one hand on her head and the other on her belly.

"Come on, Leila, sit," Christa instructed, handing her a bottle of water.

Leila took it, flopped down on the sofa, and let out a huff. "I just feel . . ." Another tear fell.

"Relax, girl. Take a deep breath and tell me what's going on," she said.

"All I can think about is my bookstore, and all Ray has for me is how great it will be for me to become this supermom and wife. I love my family, Christa; you know that. I love my man, and my kids are my world, but do you know how good it felt to open my bookstore? As bad as my marriage was with Devon, he was behind me 110 percent when I decided to open my store." She paused and gulped her water. She took a few deep breaths and continued, "And now, all that work is just down the drain."

"Leila, I understand, hon, but you can't stress and dwell on it. You are going to be okay without the store. You didn't fail, and at least you got to do something you wanted to do. Not all people can say that."

"I know, Christa, but what if your agent called you tomorrow and said your modeling career was over, and nobody wants you to model their clothes, makeup, or shoes, or see that beautiful smile on a billboard?" When Christa looked down and didn't say anything, Leila said, "Exactly. See, that is how I feel. I know I'm a good mother and a great wife, and I was that when I had my bookstore."

"I know, Lei, but you have to get out of this rut. I hear you. It would absolutely kill me if I got that call, but I would be able to say I did what I set out to do, and so can you. You can do other things. This doesn't mean life's over."

"I know, Christa, it's just going to take some time to get over it." She swallowed more water.

They sat in silence for a moment or two, and then Christa spoke again. "Leila, I need to ask you something," she said shyly.

"What is it?" Leila asked, turning to face her.

"If this makes you uncomfortable, please just tell me, but I need to know."

"What, Christa? Spit it out."

"Well, it's about Devon and me—"

"Oh no, don't even ask for any inside info about Devon. That, my dear, you are going to have to experience on your own," she said, standing and moving toward the window. Christa loved her view and hardly ever closed the curtains, so she knew why Leila gravitated to Chicago's lakeshore view.

"Come on, Leila. You're the only person I can ask and, not only that, but also, I know you'll be honest with me." She followed Leila to the window.

"No, Christa, I don't want to get into your and Devon's business. It's freaky enough that you guys somehow hit it off. No," Leila said, putting up her hands.

"You talk to me all the time about you and Ray."

"Yes, and you and Ray never hooked up. Or is there something you and Ray failed to mention?" She tilted her head to the side, giving Christa a suspicious stare.

"No, no, no. Come on. You know that nothing ever happened between us." She saw the tension in Leila's forehead ease. "All I want to know is one thing," she pleaded.

Leila sighed. "Okay, Christa, come on," she said reluctantly. "What do you want to know?"

"How is Devon in bed?" she blurted out.

Leila laughed out loud. "That is *not* a question that you should be asking me," Leila said, smiling and shaking her head.

"Why not? We're friends."

"And Devon and I were married. I can't discuss our sex with you." Leila walked back toward the sofa.

Christa followed her. "You tell me about your sex with Rayshon, Leila."

"Ummm, hello? That's different. You can't compare the two." Leila flopped down on the couch. "This is crazy and so comical. I'm going to need a shot of something to have this conversation with you, Christa, because talking about Ray and me is totally different."

"How? We're girlfriends, Leila, and you tell me about sex with Ray, and I have told you about other guys I've dated, so why can't we talk about sex with Devon?"

"Because it's weird, Christa, and it makes me uncomfortable to think about you and Devon and sex."

Christa sat down on the ottoman across from Leila. "Why? You guys have been over for years now, and you have watched Devon see other women. And you're the only person I can ask."

"Look, why don't you ask Devon or, better yet, just have sex with him? And," Leila added, holding up one finger, "when you do, I don't care to hear about it."

"Are you kidding me?" Christa asked in disbelief.

"No, I'm serious."

"Well, I will put that in my mental Rolodex, but I can't promise you I won't spill. I wanna have sex with him, Leila, but it's like he's afraid to have sex with me."

"Afraid?" Leila burst into laughter. "You are *so* funny. I haven't laughed this hard in weeks, girl. It may be something, Christa, but fear isn't it. I know Devon way too well. When we were good, the sex was outstanding." She stopped talking, and Christa realized she'd gone back to her original plan of not discussing sex about her ex-husband.

"So, what can it be?" she asked, hoping Leila knew something. She and Devon had been dating for five months, and the only passion they shared were passionate kisses that led them nowhere.

"Christa, I don't know."

"Can you find out? Can you talk to him for me, please?" Christa pleaded.

"Are you high, Christa? No, I *can't* talk to him about why he's not doing you," Leila said, looking at her as if she were crazy.

"Come on, Leila, you and Devon are friends, and I really like him. I know y'all have some bad history, but you guys are good now, and I know he'll talk to you."

"No, Christa, absolutely not. I don't want to get involved or in the middle of your and Devon's sex life. Just talk to him."

"I've tried, but he avoids the conversation. I like him, Leila."

"Well, Christa, you're going to have to figure out something, because it's weird enough as it is that you and Devon are together. I do *not* want to hear a word about the two of you naked between the sheets or in the shower or on the kitchen counter, you hear me? No matter how hot the story is, I *don't* wanna hear it."

"Damn, Devon gets down like that?" Christa asked, wondering if that's how he used to do her.

"Eeeew. No, Christa, that's how Rayshon and I do it," Leila said and laughed.

"Oh shit, I was gonna say," Christa said, and they both laughed.

"Well, I'm not talking about Devon's ass."

"I wish you were," Christa said and slapped her thigh.

"Give him time. He and I do have some bad history, and we went through a very rough patch, but he's a great father, and deep down, he's a good person. He just got stupid on me." Leila laughed. "Shit, it wasn't funny back then, but now I'm able to laugh about it."

"I guess you're right." Christa sat for a moment or two before she went back to Leila's original reason for coming over. "So, I heard Ray's new spot opened several days ago."

"Yep," Leila replied and smirked a little. "Gym number three."

"That's awesome for you guys. I remember meeting Ray at the old gym he used to work at before he converted his loft. This has always been his dream, and he's doing it."

"Yep, he is," Leila said, standing to leave. "Look, I'm going to head back to the house. I walked out on Ray after an argument."

"Leila, you will feel better. Soon, the baby will be here, and you will have something to do," Christa said, and then wished she hadn't.

"My baby isn't gonna replace my store, Christa," Leila said, moving toward the door.

"I know, Lei, and I didn't mean it that way."

"I know, Christa, and thanks for listening. I'll call you tomorrow." Leila walked out without giving Christa a chance to say good night.

Chapter Four

Ray proudly walked into the gym, but he felt horrible about what Leila was going through. He didn't have a clue how he was going to make her feel better. He wished that he could have flooded her store with tons of customers every day to keep her business going strong like he was. Every time he walked into that store, it reminded him of the day that they met. That store meant a lot to him too, but he didn't have a solution to save it for her, something he had secretly tried doing by making sure he had flyers and posters hung all over his gym advertising her promotions, sales, and events.

Sadly, the store's profit dropped drastically, and it wasn't making enough money even to cover the utilities. Leila did everything she could. She also brought in authors from all over to increase sales in the store. The headliners always had a great turnout, but they were the most expensive to bring in. She thought about moving the store to a different location, but after she got pregnant, she didn't bring up that idea anymore. As the store became slower and slower, she had to let her oldest and most reliable employee, Nikki, go, and when her best friend Renee finished school, she was okay with not working at the store anymore. She took a position out of state, and she and Leila still talked but not as much as they did when Renee first left.

Ray was stressed enough with trying to get his businesses going, so he dove into his projects to avoid hearing Leila cry and moan about the store. He wanted her happy and would give his life for her happiness, but when it came to that bookstore, there was nothing he could say or do right, and it caused him and Leila to argue more than they ever argued before. He truly understood that it had to hurt, but he figured she was smart and talented and could find something else that she loved to do. And taking care of him and the kids should have been a job she wanted to accept gladly, he told himself, but obviously, that wasn't what made her content.

He reached for his roster to see his new schedule. He hadn't done any personal training sessions in a while due to him expanding and was happy that this facility was finally up and functioning so he could get back to doing what he loved. After he looked over his list of back-to-back appointments, he ran into his office to call Leila before he started. The last couple of days had been quiet, and she had barely spoken to him since the night she walked out on their argument.

"Hey, babe, I hope you're feeling better today. I have a full schedule, but you know if you need me at any moment, they can page me. Try to get out today, babe. Take a walk in the park or something. I just don't want you moping. I love you, baby, and I want you to feel better," he said and hung up. He got up and headed to the floor to see who this new client Karen was. His mouth dropped open when he saw her. It was Karen, the nurse. The Karen he'd never called back.

"Hello, Rayshon," she said.

"Karen, it's been a long time," he said nervously, wondering if she was over the fact that he never called her back after lying to her about hooking up with her again. She had called him several times, and he never answered because he and Leila had gotten together.

"It certainly has," she said.

He didn't know how to read her expression. "How have you been?"

"Good, really good. I'm now a licensed RN, and I work at the hospital across the street. I was counting down the days for you guys to open, and when I came in, I learned that you owned the place." She gave him a bright smile. "Congratulations."

"Thank you, and you are my first client, so we should get started. I see your profile is already filled out, so follow me," he said.

He wanted to get straight to the workout and not talk too much. After she did her warmup, he moved over to the mat and began giving her some basic instructions on the exercise they were about to do.

"I'm not bitter about you not calling me," she announced suddenly.

Although he was relieved, he absolutely didn't want to talk about that. "Yeah, well, I'm very happy to hear that you're not. We wouldn't be able to be in our one-hour sessions if you still harbored some old anger."

"Well, I'm over it. It's wasn't like you and I kicked it that long. After a few weeks of checking my phone every five minutes, waiting on your call, and dealing with the fact that you were no longer answering my calls, I put you in the one-night stand compartment."

He wondered if her tone was that of someone really over it or someone still harboring some old feelings. "One-night stand? We did it again the next morning, remember?" he said, trying to make a joke of it.

She gave him a little laugh that sounded a little more convincing that she was over it. "You are so right, and it was wonderful."

Ray decided just to agree and go back to the treadmill so they could stop talking. When the session was over, Karen gave him a friendly smile.

"Well, Rayshon Johnson, it was a pleasure to see you again. It's been, what, almost six years, and you're still as handsome as ever."

"Thank you, and you are just as gorgeous as you were the night we met. I'm going to be real with you. When I met you, it was bad timing. I was already feeling someone, but to be totally honest, I didn't know if I had a chance with her. Now, six years later, we're married, two kids, and another coming soon."

"Wow, that's great," she said and nodded. She smiled and told him she'd see him next week.

As soon as she was on the other side of the door, he rushed to call his best friend, Mario.

"Man, you will never guess who just left," he said. He wondered what was going on in Karen's little head. She seemed to be cool, but he couldn't determine if she really was.

"Who, crazy-ass Katrina?" Mario joked, laughing out loud.

"Man, hell no. And why would you say her name? You know that name gives me the shakes."

"My bad, man," Mario said. "Hold on, let me shut my office door. My new assistant is always walking back and forth in front of my door, giving me that look, and I'm not trying to get fired or killed, ya hear me?"

"I feel you. I know those types all too well, but, dude, *Karen* was my first appointment today," Ray said.

"Karen Karen Karen . . . Who in the hell is Karen?"

"You remember that chick I hooked up with right before Leila and I got together? She was out that night with her girl Logan, Lisa, or Leslie—whatever that damn girl's name was. The nurses, the one I told you to ditch before Linda had your ass on the six o'clock news."

"Oh yeah, that short chick with a whole lot of cleavage and a very little ass," Mario recalled.

"Yes, her. And you remember how I played her to the left, then she showed up to my place unannounced, and I promised to call her and never did? She called me for like a month or two after that, but Leila and I had hooked up, and I wasn't feeling her."

"Okay, so what's the bottom line, man?" Mario asked.

"Well, I think she is still ill about it," he said.

Mario burst into laughter. "Dawg, I know you are fine-ass Rayshon Johnson," he teased, "with the broad shoulders and eight-pack abs, but why would she still be thinking about your ass after what, six years? Your son is four, and you met her before Leila even got pregnant, man. Yo' ass ain't that irresistible."

"You know what, man? You're right. No way is she still tripping about that after all this time. Hell, she probably dating a doctor or some shit. I'm trippin', dude. I have to get back to work. Thanks, man."

"Anytime," Mario said.

"Are we still on for drinks tonight?"

"Yes. Let's meet up at Club Jay's. I heard they do karaoke on Wednesday or some shit."

"Karaoke, dude?"

"Yes, and they have two-dollar drink specials. You know Linda was laid off. I can't be splurging like yo' rich ass."

"Man, whatever. I'll meet you there at eight," Ray said and hung up. He tried Leila again, but she didn't answer, and he didn't leave another message.

Hours later, Rayshon tried Leila once more—for the fifth time—before he went inside Jay's to meet Mario. She still didn't answer. He wanted to go home and check on her, but he didn't want to deal with her right then. He just wanted to clear his mind. He walked in, spotted Mario, and went to join him. They talked in between karaoke performances when they could actually hear what each other was saying. He turned around on his stool when he heard them announce Kennedy Roberson, the owner of KBanks Jewelers, and a friend of Leila's, and watched the woman who had just sold him a piece of jewelry for his wife the other day make her way to the stage. He hadn't known she was a singer. He applauded with everyone else after she was done giving them her version of Jill Scott's "A Long Walk." Then he hurried over to say hello.

"Kennedy," he said.

She turned to him. "Mr. Johnson, how are you?"

"I'm good, and please, call me Ray. Wow, what a voice. Why are you a jeweler?" he joked.

"Because that's what I love doing. This here is something my husband loves to watch me do, so every now and then, I grace the stage with my presence."

At that moment, Julian walked up. "Ray, right?" he asked.

"Oh, wow, Julian, right? You work out at my gym near your restaurant."

"Yeah, and your wife owned that bookstore a couple of doors down, right?"

"Yes, but, of course, you know it's no longer in business."

"Damn, I'm sorry, man. That's unfortunate."

"Yep, we just hope it sells fast."

"You're trying to sell the space?" Kennedy asked. Ray nodded. "Well, I have just the person you need to meet. Hold on,'" she said and rushed off. Moments later, she reappeared with another woman.

"Mr. Johnson, this is my best friend, Cherae Brooks, and she just happens to be a talented real estate agent."

"Hi, Cherae. Very nice to meet you, but we already have an agent. Sorry."

"Well, I think you'll be sorrier if you don't fire your agent and hire me," Cherae said with confidence.

"Really? Cherae, I'll have to talk it over with my wife, and if she says so, then you are as good as hired," he said.

Cherae handed him a card. "Great! I look forward to hearing from you soon, Mr. Johnson. It was nice to meet you," she said and walked away.

"Well, Ray, I have to get back to work." Julian turned to Kennedy. "Babe, don't forget to go up to my office and put the order in for the bar. We can't be outta liquor this weekend," he said and gave her a quick kiss.

"Okay, baby, I'll go up in a second," she said. "So, how did Leila like the necklace?" she asked Ray after watching her husband walk away.

"Aw, she loved it. It's just I'm not her favorite person right now."

"Don't worry, it's going to take a minute to settle with the idea that the business is gone, but she won't stay this way forever."

"I hope not," he said, rubbing his head.

"She won't. Now, go to the bar, tell Tony that I said your drinks are on the house, and you relax your mind, Ray."

"Thanks again, Kennedy."

"You're welcome."

Ray watched her head to a flight of stairs that had a sign that said: "*Management Only*." He went back to the bar and hung out with Mario for a little while longer, and then he headed home. When he got there, the kids were sleeping, but he stole a few kisses from them both.

He found Leila in the bathroom. "I called you several times today," he said, standing in the doorway. Leila was soaking in the tub and massaging her stomach with bath oil.

"I know." She didn't look up.

"Are you going to continue to do this to yourself, Leila? You know this stress is not good for the baby," he said, wanting to suck all of her pain out of her.

"If I hear that one more damn time," she yelled, throwing her hands up.

Ray was so frustrated that he walked away. He went downstairs, grabbed the rum and a glass from the cabinet, and took two back-to-back shots. He saw the message light on the phone blinking and hit *play*. After the first four messages from him, there was one from her OB/ GYN, Dr. Bryce.

"Leila, you missed your appointment today. I told you until we can get your blood pressure under control, we need to see you twice a week. Give us a call right away to set up another appointment."

Rayshon slammed the glass on the counter and raced upstairs, taking two steps at a time. Leila jumped when he stormed into the bathroom.

"What the fuck, Leila? What, baby? What the hell are you trying to do—kill yourself? Kill the baby? Baby, I'll get you another bookstore. Hell, I'll convert every gym I have into a bookstore if you want, but please, stop this, Leila." Tears burned his eyes. "You didn't tell me that your blood pressure was up again. You didn't tell me that Dr. Bryce said for you to see him twice a week," he yelled, holding up two fingers. He was so mad that he wanted to shake her. "And why did you miss your appointment today?"

Leila didn't answer. She just stared at the bottle of bath soap on the side of the tub with glossy eyes.

"Baby, I don't know what else to say or do," he said, moving closer to her. "I love you, Leila, with everything. And right now, all I care about is your health and the baby. You will go in to see Dr. Bryce tomorrow, and until our baby is delivered, you will do whatever he tells you," he declared and walked away. He slammed the front door so loud, he was sure it echoed through the entire house, but he didn't care. He was beyond angry, and he didn't try to hide it.

Chapter Five

Leila sat in the waiting room, trying to remain as calm as possible so that her blood pressure would be normal. Rayshon had driven her to the doctor's office, and he hadn't said one word to her the entire ride. In fact, he hadn't said more than two words to her that morning. When Dr. Bryce examined Leila, Rayshon smiled at the news that her pressure was normal, but Dr. Bryce made her set up an appointment for the following week anyway. She had four more weeks before she was due to deliver, and he wanted to make sure Leila made it and that she and the baby were healthy.

When they got home, Rayshon got out and helped her out of the passenger seat, but when they got inside, he kept his distance from her.

When he had to go to the gym, he went up to tell her he was leaving. "I'm heading to the gym to finish up my last four sessions, and then I'll be straight home. I'll pick up some takeout, so don't worry about dinner. I just want you to rest," he said and turned to walk away.

"Ray," Leila called out softly, so low he barely heard her.

"Yeah?" he said and stopped and turned back to her.

"I'm sorry," she said. Her voice was low and hoarse. "I don't want to hurt our baby."

He came back into the room and sat on the bed with her. "I know, Lei. I want to fix it. I want to take away your pain, but you gotta try too, Leila, and stop wallowing in it."

"I know," she whispered.

He held her tightly. "It's just a store." He felt her body tense.

"If I had a dollar for every time someone told me that," she mumbled. Ray didn't respond. He just held her close. "I'm going to rest now," she said.

He kissed her softly on the lips. "I love you, baby," he said and wiped her cheek.

"I know, and I love you too," Leila said. "Now, go and finish up."

Ray got up and left. When she heard the door close, she sobbed uncontrollably into her pillow. She cried until she fell asleep.

The ringing of her phone woke her, and she realized her family wasn't home yet. She looked at the caller ID. It was Christa.

"Hello," Leila answered.

"Hey, hon, I have a question," Christa said cheerfully.

"What is it?"

"What's Devon's favorite food?"

"Christa, you've *got* to be kidding me."

"Come on, Leila. I want to make a nice, romantic dinner here at my place, and I want to surprise him."

"Christa, I told you that I don't want to be in your and Devon's mix."

"You said we couldn't discuss *sex*. You never said food."

Leila shook her head. "Fried chicken," she answered, "with homemade mac and cheese, green beans, and corn muffins."

"What? I don't know how to make that."

"Well, that's his favorite meal to eat, Christa. He loved for me to make that when we were happy."

"Shit. I don't know how to make soul food, Leila. What do I do?"

"Grab something from Dusty's. I don't know," she suggested.

"It won't be the same, Leila, please help me. Come over and show me how to make it."

"Christa, I don't want to make food for my ex-husband and his new girlfriend. Google it. I'm sure you can follow a recipe."

"I know you hate this, but all of my friends, besides you, are models and wouldn't dare touch fried chicken, mac and cheese, or corn muffins. I really like Devon, Leila. I know he's your ex, but you're the only friend I have who can cook, and you're the only friend I have who knows how to make my man's favorite food. Please, Leila?" she begged.

Leila sighed. She didn't want to do it. "Okay," she finally said.

"Oh, thank you, Leila. Thank you. I want to do it on Sunday. Please email me all the things I need, and I'll be ready."

"Okay, Christa, and after this, nothing else when it comes to you and Devon. I mean it."

"Okay," Christa said happily.

They hung up, and Leila made her way downstairs. It was only a little after five, and she still had over an hour before anyone would be home. She went to the fridge to get something to drink and saw Cherae's business card. She wondered what Ray was up to with a realtor's business card. He hadn't discussed buying or selling anything. She grabbed it and called.

"Cherae Brooks," Cher answered.

"Mrs. Brooks?" Leila said.

"Yes, how can I help you?"

"Well, I'm not sure. My name is Leila Johnson, and I just came across your card. I was wondering, do you know my husband, Rayshon Johnson?"

"Oh, yes, of course. I met him through a friend of mine, Kennedy Roberson. She said she used to get all of her books from your store, except when the one she wanted wasn't in stock," Cher joked.

Leila didn't laugh with her. "Yeah, okay. I'm familiar with Kennedy. She also helped my husband pick out a beautiful necklace for me last week."

"Yes, she does have great taste in jewelry," Cher said.

"Well, I was just wondering, did my husband mention that we were looking to buy or sell some property?"

"Actually, it was about your store. I told him if he really wanted to get it sold, that I'd be a better fit. I know the area well, and I can almost guarantee you that it will be sold a lot faster with me as your realtor."

"Really? Did he tell you I already have a realtor?"

"Yeah, and Mr. Grant is a cool dude, but he's old and a bit rusty. And I know for a fact that he is not out there trying to get your property sold," she said and laughed again.

"Why would you say that?"

"Well, I'll tell you what. I'll email you a list to compare my closings and Mr. Grant's closings for the past six months. If you call me back, I know you're ready to sell," Cherae said confidently.

"Okay, Mrs. Brooks," Leila said.

She gave Cher her email address and went to her website. She saw that she was closer, so she decided to meet Cherae at the property the following week to do a walk-through.

Leila arrived with Christa to do the walk-through. Since she had cooked a fabulous meal for Devon, Christa agreed to go with her that morning without hesitation. Usually, Crista would decline on doing anything that wasn't all about her, but Leila knew she'd have Christa saying yes to whatever she'd ask for a while because Devon enjoyed the dinner so much.

Leila and Christa got out of the truck, and when they spotted Cherae coming up the street, Christa and Cherae stopped in their tracks when they saw each other.

"Cherae Thompson," Christa snarled.

"Christa Montgomery," Cherae snarled back.

Leila wondered what in the hell was going on. "Okay, you two know each other?" she asked.

"Unfortunately," Christa said. She narrowed her eyes at Cherae.

"Okay, Christa, this is a business meeting for me, and I'm not going to allow my personal affairs with you to alter my meeting."

"Okay, wait," Leila said, "how do you two know each other?"

"Well," Cherae said, "forgive my unprofessionalism." She put her hands on her hips. "She stole my man."

"What?" Christa asked. "Miles dumped you for me, and you weren't woman enough to walk away with class."

"No, I came home, and you had already moved in and had my stuff boxed up and out in the damn hallway. How could you do that to another woman?"

"Hold on, I'm confused," Leila said. She wanted to know the details of this drama.

Cher crossed her arms. "Well, Miss Christa, here, was my younger replacement. She moved in while I was having a spa day, and I had to move in with my best friend because of what she did."

"Yeah? And word on the street is that didn't work out too well, backstabber," Christa yelled.

"Hey, Kennedy and I are just fine," Cher said defensively.

"Yeah—now. After she kicked your sorry ass out on the streets," Christa spat.

Cher's eyes welled up with tears. "You know what, Leila? We need to reschedule." She turned to walk away.

"Wait, Cherae, wait. I don't have much time. As you can see, I am close to my due date. Can we please go inside and take care of business? Christa can stay outside."

"Yeah, sure," Cherae said. "Look, Christa, we all have a past, and mine ain't nowhere near perfect. But at least I'm woman enough to admit that I did a sister wrong, something you can't do." When Christa nodded, she continued, "We were both in the wrong. Miles was married, and you moving into my downtown condo while I was on a spa day was devious. Miles had both of us on a side-chick high at that time, and neither of us cared who we were replacing. You and I used to do the same thing—chase the men with money. But you know what you did wasn't right to his wife or me."

"You know what, Cherae? You are absolutely right. I assisted Miles in hurting you, and I apologize. And, for the record, he did the same thing to me one year later, so at least you had two years."

"Yea, I had two years, but if I had to do it all over, I'd decline both," Cher said.

They all laughed and walked inside the empty store.

After the walk-through, Cher said, "Leila, have you thought about just renting this place? I mean, it's in a great location, and with some minor upgrades, it could rent easily."

"Nah, I just want to be done."

"Are you sure?" Cherae asked.

"Wow, Leila," Christa said, "she may be on to something."

"Yeah, like what? Making this a pole-dancing school?" Leila joked.

"Well, I thought about what you said about me not being able to model anymore. The reality is, I know I won't be able to model forever. Hell, look at Cherae now. She had to get a real job. Gold digging got played out," she joked.

"Hey, watch it," Cher said.

"I have always wanted to open a modeling agency, and what better time for me to start than now? I still can do a few modeling gigs, but I know my time is passing. I want to help other young women and men do what I was fortunate to do."

Leila thought for a second. "Wow, Christa. I had no idea you wanted to do something like that. Let me run it by Ray, and then we can go from there."

"That sounds good," Cherae said.

"Well, won't that be bad for you, Mrs. Brooks?" Christa asked.

"Nope, because Christa will be the tenant, and I'll make sure it's done the correct and legal way by being your rental property manager. That way, she will be subject to the same terms as any other renter. That will save your friendship, trust me," she said.

Chapter Six

"Hey," Karen said when she saw Rayshon coming from his office. Their session was over, but she wanted to talk to him.

"Hey, Karen, what's up?"

"I just need someone to talk to right now," she said. Her eyes watered. "Do you have a minute?"

Ray hesitated but agreed. "Ummm, sure. Yeah, hold on," he said. She watched him go over and talk to his desk agent. "Come on," he said when he finished, and they walked out the door.

"Listen, my place is several blocks down. Do you mind if we go there?" she asked.

Ray paused. "Look, Karen, you know I'm married. Going to your place may not be a good idea."

"That's cool. I totally understand. We can walk across to the hospital and sit," she suggested.

"Yes, a public place would be better," he said. He followed Karen to a spot in the back of the hospital, and they sat on a bench. "So, what's wrong?" he asked.

"Everything," she said.

"Everything like what, Karen? Can you be a little more specific?"

"Wow, Rayshon. What do you think is wrong with me?"

"Nothing. You are fine, beautiful, smart, and independent."

"Well, with that said, why do you think I can't keep a man?" she asked.

"I don't think I'm qualified to answer that question. I wouldn't know how to answer that. I mean, you and I didn't date, so I don't know what guys may like or dislike about you," Ray said gently.

"Okay, then, tell me why you didn't like me, Ray."

"Karen, I told you that it wasn't you. I had already fallen for someone."

Karen didn't reply right away. "My boyfriend just sent me a text message saying it was over. That bastard had the nerve to say it was because I was too good for him."

"Okay, maybe that's his truth," Ray said.

"How can you break up with someone and tell them that they were too good for you?"

"Well, truthfully, the brother could have been being honest with you. He knows himself, and he may know that he's an asshole, or maybe he's not where you are in life, or he doesn't wanna damage you because he isn't ready to do what you're trying to do right now. Consider yourself lucky."

She smiled. "You know what? You are right, Ray. That is *exactly* why I wanted to talk to you. Because you are one of the good ones."

"Yeah, so I've been told. Someone needs to email my wife that memo."

"Trouble in paradise?"

"Man, you have no idea," he said and leaned back against the bench. "It's like every time I try to say the right thing, it's the wrong thing. And every effort I put in to make it right, it's wrong. It's wearing me out."

"Well, maybe *you* are too good for *her*," Karen suggested.

"No, Leila and I are a perfect match and just right for each other. We're just having a rough patch."

"OK. Is there anything I can do to help you through your rough patch?" She touched his leg. She knew she was being forward, but she had never completely gotten over him.

"Naw, Karen, I'm good. I need to get back. My day isn't done yet," he said and stood.

She watched him head back to the gym without slowing up for her. Then she went back into the hospital to work.

Chapter Seven

When Ray got home, it was after nine, and he was surprised to see Devon's car at his house so late. He hoped that the kids were okay. Leila hadn't called him to say anything. When he walked in, he didn't like seeing Devon massaging her feet in his lap.

"Hey, what's going on?" he asked.

"Hey, baby," Leila said, getting up and moving toward him. "Devon stopped by to bring some things for Deja."

"Yeah, it's time for me to head out now." Devon got up and went to the kitchen. He leaned in and kissed Leila on the cheek. For the first time, Ray was bothered by it. "I'll call you tomorrow, Lei," he said. "And make sure you call me if you need anything."

"Sure, Devon, and thank you," she said, giving him a warm smile.

Devon headed for the front door. "Good night, Ray," he said, leaving.

"What the hell was that?" Ray yelled when he was gone.

"What the hell was what? And why are you raising your voice?" Leila asked, looking at him as if he were crazy.

"That! You and Devon and him rubbing your damn feet!"

"Aw. Come on, Rayshon. You know that Devon helps me a lot. We were talking, and he noticed how swollen my feet were and offered to rub them," she said nonchalantly.

"Oh, really? And the '*call me if you need anything*'?"

"Ray, you *are* joking, right? I am *not* having this conversation. This is stupid," she said and walked away, heading for the steps.

"Leila, get your ass back here," he yelled.

Leila stopped in her tracks. "What?" she asked, walking back into the kitchen with her head tilted.

"Don't ever walk away again when we're having a conversation. I don't want Devon in my house, rubbing my pregnant wife's feet. If you need anything, you call *me,* not him. I don't need Devon taking care of you."

"Hold on, Rayshon. Stop it with this controlling rage. Devon and I are friends, Ray—that's it. He and I are close, yes, but he and I are over. And if he is here for me when you are too busy out running one of your damn fitness centers, that's how it's gonna be. I have two children to take care of and a baby in my womb that's stomping on the right side of my body twelve hours of the day, all while I'm dealing with the other stresses of my life, and you are in my face with this nonsense."

"Leila, don't go there. Every effort I make to help you, you push me away. Every effort I make to make you smile, you frown. Then I walk into my house and see your damn feet in your ex-husband's lap and how you give him warm smiles before he makes his exit puts my head in a bad place, Leila, when you haven't smiled at me in months," he said. He stopped when he saw the look on her face and her gripping the counter. "Baby, what's wrong?"

"I just felt something," she said.

"Baby, come sit down," he said, grabbing her arm. Suddenly, a gush of water hit the floor.

"Oh shit, Ray, my water just broke," she said, taking short quick breaths in a panic.

"I know, baby," he said. "It's everywhere."

"Call Devon," Leila said between breaths.

"What!" Rayshon yelled in disbelief.

"So he can come back and stay with the kids, Rayshon. So you can get me to the hospital," she said. She looked like she wanted to slap him.

"Yes, right," he said, scrambling for his phone. "Where is your packed bag, Lei?" he asked, pacing and scrolling through his contacts to find Devon's number.

"It's in the nursery. Look, give me the phone. You go up and get the bag and grab my sundress off the bed so I can take off these wets shorts," she instructed, and he did what she said.

"Devon, it's Lei. Please come back. My water just broke."

"I'm making a U-turn right now," Ray heard him say on speaker when he got to the top of the stairs. He hurried to grab Leila's bag and sundress. He was back so fast that Leila was still standing in the same spot.

Less than five minutes later, Devon walked in the front door. He entered the kitchen while Leila was changing. Her sundress was over her head. Ray wasn't happy about him seeing his wife naked, but his concern was more about her and the baby.

"Look, Ray, hurry and get Leila to the hospital. I got the kids," Devon said.

Ray was grateful at the moment that Devon was around. He grabbed Leila's arm and helped her out the door.

Five hours later, Leila had another little girl, and they named her Rayven. She was almost four weeks early and weighed five pounds even. After Leila was resting, Rayshon stepped into the hall and dialed Devon. He had his number, rarely used it, but he had to update him on what had happened. He needed to know if he had to call Tabitha to come, or would Devon take off the next day. Devon answered on the first ring, and Rayshon shook off the feelings of jealously that he had. Maybe Devon was just generally concerned about Leila and didn't want her back. After Devon said he could stay and take care of the kids until Leila was released, Rayshon went back into the room and picked up his little girl. She was so beautiful, and he felt blessed and decided just to trust his wife.

Chapter Eight

"So, I can't see you tonight?" Christa asked Devon, gripping her cell phone tightly. She was getting pissed. She was insane to have been saving herself for him. She was done.

"No, I have to go by Leila's and get dinner for the kids."

"You know, if I didn't know any better, I'd say that you and Leila are married instead of her and Rayshon."

"Oh, here we go again, Christa. I keep telling you that nothing's going on with Leila and me. She just had a baby, my hours are more flexible than Rayshon's, and she needs me."

"We haven't been out on a real date in almost four weeks, Devon, and *I* miss you. Don't you miss me?"

"Yes, I do. But I can't leave Leila hanging, okay? I've done enough of that in my day."

The bulb went off. "So, you still feel guilty? After all these years, you still feel guilty for what you did?"

"Come on, Christa, don't be ridiculous. Leila is my friend and the mother of my child. If we have to keep having this same old, tired conversation about her, then maybe you and I should take a break."

"Fine, Devon. It's not like I don't already feel like we're taking one anyway," she snapped.

"Hold on, Christa, I have another call," he said.

"Leila—"

"I'll call you back," Devon said.

Christa hung up and told herself to leave Devon's ass alone. She went to the freezer and grabbed her carton of Ben and Jerry's. After eating a few teaspoons, she put it back. She looked at the clock and saw that it was a little after seven. She wanted to get out, so she grabbed her purse and keys and headed for the door.

She drove to Jay's for a drink and sat at the bar. After a while, she saw Cherae and walked over and joined her.

"Is this seat taken?" she asked.

"Hey," Cherae said, "have a seat. My husband was here, but he had to run, and I'm not ready to get home yet. So . . ." She took a sip of her drink. "What's going on?"

"Man trouble, I suppose."

"Oh, no. I'm not in any position to advise on relationships. I'm too busy trying to maintain my own," Cherae giggled.

"Cherae, I'm not trying to be in your business, and you can tell me to mind my own, but I have a question."

"Go ahead, Christa. Trust, after everything that has been said about me to my face and behind my back, I can pretty much handle anything."

"Do you and Kennedy ever mention what went down? I mean, do you ever think that she may think that you still have a thing for her husband?"

Cherae paused a moment before she spoke. "Well, we did once, and that opened up some bad feelings, but we worked through it. I'll be honest and tell you I had to get some help to figure out what was wrong with me to make me want to do such a thing to my friend. I found out a lot more about myself than I cared to know, trust me," she said and chuckled. "It took some time, but Kennedy and I were finally able to trust each other again.

"I realized that I was never in love with Julian. I was just so fixated on living a life that my best friend had.

And I'm grateful to God that it's all better. Now, on the other hand, our girlfriend, Teresa, still looks at me cross-eyed, but every day, I show and prove that I have changed. Kennedy and I may never get back what we had before that entire my-best-friend-and-my-man ordeal, but we found a way to be close again. Whether she thinks I still have a thing for Julian . . . well, that's something you need to ask her." Cher took a sip of her drink.

"That's exactly what I'm gonna do," Christa said.

"OK, she's right over there," Cher said, pointing at Kennedy.

"No, I'm going to ask my friend Leila if she still has a thing for my boyfriend, Devon."

"OMG. Leila dated your boyfriend before you did?"

"Worse—they were married."

Cherae leaned in closer. "Whhhhaaaadddd? Do tell."

"The bottom line is, he's great. A great dad, charming, and spoils the hell outta me, but no sex. And to top it off, he runs to Leila's at her every beck and call."

"Well, Christa, it looks like you have to make a choice," Cherae said.

"What choice do I have?"

"Either you sit back and let your man grow closer to his ex, or you pull out your sexiest lingerie and stilettos and work your magic. And if that doesn't work, find a man that has never been involved with your friend. Trust, it will save you a world of drama." They laughed.

"I need to talk to you," a voice said.

Cherae and Christa turned around. "Katrina," they said in unison.

"What are you doing here?" Cher asked.

"We need to talk about the money you said you'd give back to me for burying our mother," Katrina spat.

Christa's mouth dropped open. "This is your sister?" she asked Cherae.

"Unfortunately, yes," Cherae said, standing up. "Katrina, I told you that your mother and I had no dealings. The Banks raised me. Your mother disowned me when I was 7 and left me to be raised by my best friend's mother because she loved crack more than me."

"I don't know what you remember about Mom, but she wasn't always like that. She got herself together and left drugs alone for many years before she died. And even when she got herself together, you thought you were too good for us and was ashamed of your own blood. But, news flash, Cherae, you are a *Thompson*, not a Banks." She got in Cherae's face. "So, get your head outta Kennedy's ass and give me what you owe me," Katrina said.

One of the bouncers rushed over. "Cher, is everything cool?" he asked.

"Yes, everything's cool. I just need you to show this young lady to the door," she said.

Christa watched the security man look at Katrina. His face read: *Don't make this hard.*

"Don't touch me. I will go, but you *will* see me again, Cher. Trust and believe," she said and stormed out.

"My God, that girl is a thorn in my damn side," Cher said and sat back down.

"Crazy Katrina is your little sister?" Christa asked.

"Yes. Damn, and how do you know her?"

"Ummm, she tried to sabotage Leila and Rayshon's relationship a few years back. I can't believe this. I gotta call Leila," Christa replied, going for her phone. "I'll see you, Cher," she said and hurried out the door.

Chapter Nine

Leila heard her phone ringing, but she was too tired to move to get it. Between the baby not sleeping at night and dealing with the kids all day because school was out, she thought she was going to die from exhaustion. Ray had back-to-back-to-back clients, so if it weren't for Devon, she wouldn't have any help. She had made the worst mistake of her life by allowing Tabitha to take the summer off. She had figured she could deal with her own children for at least the summer, but they were only four weeks in, and she couldn't.

She finally turned over and mustered up the strength to see who had been calling her. It was Christa. She didn't want to talk to her. Devon had told her about her accusing them of having something more than a friendship. Why Devon was celibate or not sleeping with Christa was a conversation she didn't want to have with him, because, frankly, it wasn't any of her business.

She put the phone on the nightstand and realized the house was extremely quiet. She got up and went to the bathroom and checked on the baby, sleeping in her bassinette before going downstairs. No one was there. She scratched her head. She remembered going up to nurse the baby while Devon stayed downstairs with the kids. He must have just taken them out for a while. She grabbed the cranberry juice from the fridge just as Devon and the kids walked in. He was carrying RJ, who was sleeping. Deja's eyes were heavy.

"I'm gonna take him up and get Deja into bed," Devon whispered.

"Thank you so much, Devon. I appreciate everything," she said.

When he came back down, Leila was loading the dishwasher.

"How are you feeling, Lei?" he asked.

"Fine, Devon. I'm fine."

"How are you *really* doing, Leila?"

She leaned back against the sink and took a deep breath. "I feel like shit." Tears filled her eyes.

"Aw, Lei, don't cry," he said, moving toward her.

She put a hand up to stop him. She had more to say. "I-I-I-I never saw this coming, you know? I had a vision of what my life would be, and it's like a bunch of bad writers who have it in for me hijacked the movie. Why is this not us? I mean, I married you, Devon, to have a family. My store . . . And all that went up in smoke."

"Leila, you know how sorry I am," he said.

She cut him off. She didn't need his sorry anymore. "I know you are, Devon, and you don't have to apologize anymore. I know you're sorry every day when you come here and make sure I'm okay and that the kids are okay. I know you're sorry. I love Rayshon, Devon. My heart is with him right now, but I will be so honest and say there are a lot of things about you that I miss. And yes, I have moments when I ask myself, 'What if I were still with Devon?' And then I think of Ray and how awesome and loving and caring he is. I know he loves me, but he just can't feel my pain the way he used to. I can't be mad at him about that anymore. I have to figure me out and find something else that will give my life some fulfillment because if I don't, I'm gonna go crazy."

She started to sob, and Devon pulled her into his arms. He held her tightly while she cried. When he let her go, she looked up. Rayshon stood watching them. From his expression, it was best for Devon to leave.

"Look, Leila, I'll talk to you later," Devon said and headed for the door.

When he left, Leila and Rayshon stood in the kitchen, looking at each other. Leila dried her face and went back to the dishes.

"You can't talk to me now, Leila? Is Devon who you want and need? Is *that* it? Now you wanna go back to him?"

"No, Ray," she replied. "No."

"Then what am I supposed to do? I can't tell him to stay away from my house because his daughter lives here, but I can't keep watching you and him carry on like he's still your husband. *I* am your husband."

"Rayshon, Devon is just a good friend to me and a good father to Deja. He helps me. That is it, baby. I love you, Ray. That hasn't changed. Have circumstances changed in this marriage to make us different? Yes. But I'm still here, and I'm still your wife." She moved closer to him and put her head on his chest.

Ray wrapped his arms around her. There were no more words to be spoken. It had been weeks since he felt the heat from her body. He planted a few kisses on her forehead and then made his way down to her lips.

His dick hardened and started to ache. They hadn't made love in months, and he realized at that moment just how much he really missed her. He grabbed her ass and pressed as hard as he could against her body, and she moaned.

"Baby, I've missed you. I want you," he said.

Leila reached into his sweats and grabbed his erection. She hadn't touched it in so long, and the way it stiffened so fast, she knew that he was happy to feel her touch.

"Follow me," she said.

They rushed into the family room. Leila sat on the coffee table and pulled his sweats down to expose his erection, then took him inside of her mouth. He grabbed her head and held it gently as his rod glided in and out of her mouth. She grabbed it and traced the tip of his head with her tongue, making his body jerk, and he squirted in her face.

Leila looked up and smiled at him, and she felt the connection they used to have. "Let me get you a towel, baby. I'm sorry for that, but you know how good you are," he said, putting his nut-tipped penis back into his boxers. He hurried off and got her a hot towel, and when he handed it over, she wiped her face.

As soon as she put the towel down, the baby monitor released the sounds of the baby crying, so Leila got up.

"I'm not done with you yet, Leila," he said when she got closer to the stairs.

She paused and turned back to him. "I hope not," she said and smiled before going upstairs.

Chapter Ten

Leila parked and took a few deep breaths before opening her door. She was ready to see what her bookstore had transformed into since Christa had become her renter. Christa had been blowing her phone up for the last couple of days, and Leila was still a little irked at her for saying she and Devon had something more than what it was. Friendship and that's it, Leila thought as she took Rayven's stroller out of the back of her Armada.

Deja was with Devon, and Rayshon had taken RJ to work with him. He had told Leila that he'd just let him go to the gym's daycare to give her a little peace. It was cool, but Leila didn't like the idea of her son being in one room all day. After Rayshon assured her that he would let him hang out with him between sessions, she had given in.

"Hello, hello, hello," Leila said as she entered what was once her bookstore. She looked around in awe because the space seemed so different, and it was beautiful.

"Leila," Christa said with excitement, "come on in. I've been calling you, girl. I know you are buried in children, but could you have at least answered one call or called a sister back?" She reached for the baby. "Aw, li'l Rayven is so beautiful," she said, picking her up out of her stroller. "She should be my first little client."

"Girl, I'm sorry. Half the time, I don't even know where my phone is. The kids are driving me bananas. It looks so good in here. Oh my, paint and wood floors go a long way." Leila missed her bookstore even more.

"Yes, it's turning out so lovely. This place is so great. I haven't even put up the new sign yet, and I already have folks tapping on the window asking me when I open."

"Wow, that is so great, Christa. I'm happy for you." Leila walked around, admiring the new accents that had been added. Modern sconces, mirrors, art, and beautiful images of Christa from her modeling days made the room look like a modeling agency.

"Rayven is so pretty, Leila. You should consider letting her model."

Leila knew she had a gorgeous baby, but she was not interested in making her into a baby model. "Hey, Rayven is not going to be your first client, so stop. She is too little to have cameras in her face."

"You say that, but I know somebody that works for Gerber. Rayven could be the next Gerber Baby." Christa tickled Rayven under her little neck, and the baby smiled. "See, look at that beautiful smile."

"Again, no thanks. Rayven is not ready for the spotlight," Leila said, moving to the back of the store to what used to be her office. "Wow, you changed everything in here too." She felt a pang. She didn't realize that to see the changes to her store was going to hurt like this.

"Yeah, the carpet was old, and the wood throughout makes it more modern." Christa put the baby back into her stroller. "So, Leila, how have you been?"

"Good. Still telling myself to take it one day at a time, so I'm doing good. I'm looking around this place, and I don't even recognize it. But it looks great, and I hope it brings you way more success than it brought to me," she said sadly.

"Come on, now, Leila, don't go there. Don't start." Christa smiled. "Everything is going to go the way it's supposed to go, okay?"

"Okay, okay," Leila said, smiling with her.

"Now, let's get to other business. I've been blowing your phone up, Mrs. Johnson, because the other night, I found out some craziness, and I had to tell you."

"What?" Leila walked over and took a seat on a pretty red plush sofa.

"Brace yourself," Christa warned.

"Come on, girl, spill it."

"Well, your rental manager slash real estate agent is the older sister to ol' girl, Katrina."

"Katrina? Crazy Katrina that almost caught a beat-down in Ray's loft the last time I saw her ass?"

"Yep, that's the one," Christa said and sat on a stool.

"No fucking way. Are you serious?"

"Yes. The other night, I went to Jay's, and I was talking to Cherae and *bam!* Outta the blue, she walked up to Cherae with some nonsense about owing her money for burying their mother. And get this—their momma was apparently on crack, which is why Cher left home."

"Who gives a damn about their momma being on crack? The point is the woman that is handling business for me is the sister of the woman who hates me and wants my man."

"*Wanted* your man. And speaking of wanting men . . ." Christa took a deep breath. "Do you still want Devon?"

"Excuse me?" Leila asked. Christa had to be on crack too, to think that. "That's absurd, Christa."

"No, it isn't. I don't know what kinda hold you have on Devon, but it's affecting our relationship."

"Christa, listen to yourself. Whatever issues you have with Devon have absolutely nothing to do with me." Leila was pissed. How dare Christa come out of her mouth saying something so ridiculous.

"Well, it has to be something, and I decided to be up front and ask."

"Well, you are barking up the wrong tree. Whatever is wrong or not right with you and Devon is between you and Devon. Like I told you before, Devon and I are close friends, and that may never change. If that's a problem for you, maybe you should consider leaving one of us alone."

"What?" Christa asked and stood up.

"You heard me, Christa. I mean, I get so tired of telling you and telling Ray over and over that nothing is going on with Devon and me. Yet, you blame me for Devon not sleeping with you. If that's making you so unhappy, then dump his ass."

"You'd love that, wouldn't you?" Christa spat.

Leila was speechless. "Well, I thought you were more than just a pretty face, but I guess I was wrong. Be sure that your rent is on time." She pushed the stroller toward the door.

"No worries, Leila. Devon already cut me a check," Christa yelled.

"Hey, Ray, you got a second?" Christa asked, barging into his office.

"Ummm, I guess I do since you're here," he said.

She took a seat. "I think Leila and Devon have something going on that they are not telling us."

Ray sat back and frowned. "What? What makes you say that?"

"Well, to be honest with you, Ray, Devon, and I have never had sex."

"So, you come in here assuming he's having sex with my wife?"

"I can't say that for sure, but it's something. It's like Leila can snap her fingers, and he drops everything to rush to her side."

"Christa, it sounds like you're a little jealous of their friendship."

"Ya think? I don't know, Ray. At times, I feel like it's more than that. I notice the way he looks at her and how he is like this good guy when she's in the room. And I swear, as sweet as Devon is to me, I don't think that he's really into me. I mean, not like he's into Leila."

"Listen, Christa, you need to talk and confront Devon with what you're feeling. But trust me, I know my wife, and she isn't sleeping with him." He stood up. "I have work to do. I've got a client waiting," he said and left.

"Well, Rayshon, I hope you're right," she said.

Chapter Eleven

"Hey, Devon," Leila said when he walked in.

"Hey, how are you, beautiful?"

"I'm fine, but we need to talk," she said.

He set the Chinese food he brought for her and the kids on the counter. "Okay."

Leila told Deja to take her brother upstairs. When they were gone, she turned to Devon. "Look, I know it's none of my business, and you can tell me to butt out if you want to, but I have to ask." She paused, nervous. "Why are you not sleeping with Christa?"

"Wow. Well, Christa and I sleep together all the time," he said.

Leila knew he knew what she meant, but she rephrased the question. "Okay, then, I'll be blunt. Why are you not fucking Christa?" she asked. She knew she was crossing the line, but she wanted Christa to understand that it had absolutely nothing to do with her.

"Whoa. I guess women *do* discuss everything."

"Yes, we do, and we also point the finger and make accusations. Christa has this big thing in her head that it's because of me." She watched him closely and waited for his response.

"Really?"

"Really," she said.

"Well, to tell you the truth, Leila, part of it's true."

Leila covered her mouth. "No, Devon, no. Don't say something so crazy, okay? We're friends, dammit. Nothing more, nothing less." She became teary-eyed. She didn't want shit to be complicated.

"I know that, Lei, but I can't stand here and look you in the eye and tell you that I still don't have feelings for you. I can't get over you, no matter how I've tried. Yes, I wish I were coming home to you every day, and, yes, I miss the hell outta you, but I know you are married to Ray. And I don't bother you with my feelings or tell you how much I hate that I fucked up our marriage and how Christa doesn't arouse me the way you do." He moved closer to her, and she stood frozen. "Leila, I miss your scent, your cooking, your singing in the shower, and having you to myself." He kissed her on the lips, and she stood there like a statue.

"No," she whispered, barely loud enough for her to hear her own voice. "We are friends," she tried to say in a normal voice.

"I know," he whispered and kissed her again. "We will always be friends, Lei, and I respect you and your marriage. I would never ask for anything more."

He moved as if to kiss her again—and Ray walked in. Devon quickly stepped aside. "Do you want me to fix the kids' plates?" he asked.

"Naw, I got it from here," Ray said.

"Okay, then, I'll be leaving." Devon hurried to the door and left.

Ray's temple flared. "Leila," he said through clenched teeth.

"Yes," she said, moving around the kitchen, not giving him any eye contact.

"What did I walk in on?"

"Nothing, Rayshon," she said and got two plates from the cabinet for the kids.

"Nothing?" he asked again. He sounded furious.

"Yes, nothing," she said. She went to the stairs and called the kids down.

She turned and saw Ray looking at her with disgust. Without saying anything else, he walked out the door, slamming it hard enough to shake the walls. She ran to the door and called out to him, but he kept walking toward his truck.

"Ray, wait, please!" she yelled.

He climbed into the driver's seat of his SUV without responding. Her heart raced. She didn't know what he had heard or how much he had seen. What she did know was that she had to keep her distance from Devon. She didn't want him back, and she did not want to lose Ray, either.

She decided she'd give him a little time to cool off, but when it was after midnight, and he hadn't come back home, she called him. He didn't answer, so she called again, over and over. When he still didn't answer, she texted him, asking him just to call and let her know that he was safe. He didn't reply.

Finally, close to two a.m., when she was up feeding the baby, she heard the door chime from the alarm. She was relieved that he was home.

When he walked into the room, he didn't say a word. He went straight to the master bathroom and turned on the shower. Leila sat nursing Rayven and looking into her little eyes. They were just like Ray's. Leila smiled at her. "Please tell your daddy not to be angry with me," she whispered. She wished Rayven could speak. Maybe if she told him, he'd listen.

When Ray came back into the room, she was done feeding the baby and had her sitting on her lap, patting her back for her to burp. He had a towel wrapped around him, and when he stood in front of his dresser, Leila remembered staring at his beautiful back the day they had their first sexual encounter. It was amazing then and even more amazing now because it belonged to her.

She smiled, but when he turned around with a sad look on his face, her smile faded. Their eyes locked, and he quickly looked away. He stepped into his boxers and climbed into bed. He lay on his side, facing them and began talking to the baby. He didn't say anything to Leila.

"I'm sorry," she whispered. She waited for Rayshon to reply, but he kept talking to Rayven. "Baby—"

He cut her off. "Don't, Leila, okay? Not right now."

"Then when?"

"Leila, you know—I just don't want to hear your voice right now."

That cut her deeply, and she felt a surge of pain in her stomach and heart.

"I'm sorry, Ray. Baby, listen, I know why you are mad," she said.

He stopped playing with Rayven. "You know, Leila? Do you *really* know? Or are you going tell me what you think I want to hear so that I can continue to allow you and Devon to rekindle your relationship?"

"What? Ray, Devon and I are—"

"Friends—right. Yeah, we have all heard that shit before." He sat up. "But you know what, Leila? I get it. It took a few moments to look at the big picture here. You don't have to choose. I'll choose for you. Tomorrow, I'll be talking to a lawyer to file for a legal separation. I'll move in with Mario until we can figure something out," he said and kissed the baby.

"What? Separation? What the hell, Rayshon? You're leaving me?"

"No, I'm just giving you some space to figure out what and who you want." He lay back down and turned his back to her.

"I don't need any space to figure that out, Ray. I want you. I want my marriage. I don't want Devon."

"You could have fooled me."

"Come on, baby," she said, getting up to put Rayven in her bassinet. Ray kept his back to her. She went around to his side of the bed and kneeled in front of him. "Rayshon, baby, I'm sorry, okay? I'm sorry for having Devon at the house so much. I'm sorry for calling on him when I should have been calling on you. I'm sorry if I made you feel alienated, baby. Please, I love *you,* Rayshon. I don't want you to leave. I don't want a separation. I don't want, Devon. Baby, please," she cried. "Baby, don't leave me, please," she whispered.

Ray sat up and sat on the side of the bed. Leila stood, put her arms around his neck, and pulled his head against her body. He wrapped his arms around her and held her tightly. He took a few deep breaths before he spoke.

"Leila, I love you so much, and I want to trust you. I want to believe in you, and I want to believe that you have no desire to be with your ex, but it's like every single time I turn around, I'm walking in on you and Devon embracing or him rubbing your damn shoulders or your feet, and I wonder if you stop and even think of me when you are allowing him to be there for you. I can't continue to live like this. Devon has got to get the hell outta my marriage, Lei. I mean it." He looked her in the eyes. "If you can't make the change, I'm going to make it for you."

"It's done, baby, okay? It's done. From now on, for whatever reason I would call Devon, I'll call you, okay? I'll stop having him around so much, I promise. It will only be about Deja, and I won't ever have him over, baby. Whatever it takes, I will do it, I promise. I promise. Whatever it takes, baby. I want to show you that I love you and only you," she cried and trembled.

She and Devon were over, and after what he had pulled earlier that evening, she knew keeping her distance was a must. She didn't want to lead him on or to end up in his arms like that ever again.

She held on to Ray as tightly as she could, scared to let him go. Hearing the words "separation" and "moving out" come out of his mouth made her sick to her stomach. She couldn't imagine being without him.

After she loosened the hold she had on his neck, she kissed him passionately. She pressed her body close to his, and he started to kiss her on her neck. He lifted her nightgown, pushed her panties down past her thighs, and let them drop to the floor. She pulled his erection out of his boxers, turned her back to him, and slid back and downward onto his dick.

They rocked back and forth, and she closed her eyes and bit her bottom lip as he pumped her nice and hard from the back. He held her around her waist, and she rolled her hips on him just the way he liked. He kissed her on the side of her neck, and she felt him gently nudge her forward. She leaned forward, allowing him to go deeper. She had missed him penetrating her. She missed feeling his touch, and now, more than ever, she wanted to come.

"Baby, let me get on top," she said between breaths, looking back at him.

"I'm close, and I don't want to stop," he said but then gave in. He got up and took his boxers off, and she stared at his body as if she had never seen him naked before. He slid back in the bed and rested on his elbows, waiting for her to climb aboard. She stood there, taking all of his sexiness in for a minute. Even though he didn't work out as much as he did before he opened two new gyms, his body looked amazing.

"Damn, you are sexy," she said, moving toward him.

"You are too, baby," he said.

Leila got into position with a smile. She wasn't as fit as Ray, but over the years, she had maintained her size twelve body and learned that if her husband gave her any type of compliment, he really meant it.

She reached down and grabbed his dick, eased down on him, and started slowly rolling her hips. She panted and moaned as her thighs shook from the orgasm that came so smoothly and quickly. She rested on Ray's chest, and he gave her a moment before he flipped her over to finish the job.

He didn't last three minutes before his body jerked from his climax. He looked down at Leila, and she looked up at him. She wanted him to feel the connection between them and forget about seeing Devon holding her and rubbing her feet. She knew they had a long way to go to get back to normal.

Chapter Twelve

"Mr. Vampelt, I have a Rayshon Johnson out here. Says he needs to speak with you," Devon's secretary said into the phone.

"Mr. Johnson, huh?" he said and took a deep breath. "Send him in, please." When Ray walked in, he said, "Ray, what's going on?" He knew what the conversation was going to be about, and he decided he was going to be straightforward and tell Ray the truth to his face. "What brings you by?" He hoped things didn't get out of hand.

"Devon," Ray said with a nod, "can I take a seat?"

"Sure." Devon leaned back in his office chair, waiting to hear what was on Rayshon's mind. "So, to what do I owe this visit?"

"I'll be short and brief. First, I need you to not be at my damn house every evening when I get home. Two, Leila is *my* wife, and what you are trying to do or what you think you want to do—stop it. She's my wife, Devon, *my* fucking wife, and I don't want you doing shit else for me, her, or my children. Deja is your only responsibility in my house, and she is the only person you and Leila will discuss and have communication about in the future," Ray declared.

Devon laughed inside. "Really, Ray? This is why you showed up at my office? I have no intention of ruining your marriage or making Leila unhappy. If you are so worried about our friendship, why don't you slow the fuck down and act like Leila and the kids are your priority? I mean, I get two or more calls a day from Lei with issues that you need to be handling, so the issue is not with me, Ray. You might wanna check yo' self," he said with a smirk.

"There he is," Ray said, standing. "The man who used to make my wife cry day in and day out when he was married to her. The asshole that is sitting here telling me to check myself, when he knows damn well that he is still trying to get back with the woman he ruined on the inside with fat jokes, lies, and affairs with women who intimidated her.

"You think now that you are Leila's so-called best friend that you can prey on her because her husband is out busting his ass to make sure he can continue to keep the house that she absolutely loves and to make sure that not only my kids, but *your* daughter goes to college?" Ray looked Devon straight in the eyes. "You may have fooled Leila into thinking that you are reformed and this stand-up guy, but I know your ass ain't shit, and I know you still haven't settled with the fact that Leila is not crying over your ass with a bucket of ice cream in her lap so you can come home and mentally abuse her. You had your turn, and you blew it. Now, stay the fuck away from my wife."

"Rayshon, you think you have me figured out." Devon leaned forward in his chair with a smirk on his face. "I am not preying on Leila because I think she's weak, nor do I think that you are not a great guy for busting your ass for your family. That's what a man is supposed to do. But when your wife is lonely and needs you to be there, and you can't ever break away, that makes her sad and unhappy, and I hate to see her sad or unhappy about anything. Believe it or not, Ray, I do hate the person I was when I destroyed my marriage and hurt the only woman I probably will ever love. Yes, I will be honest with you and tell you that I hate that you came to her rescue when I was a total muthafucka to my wife.

"Before I could get my act together, you were already in. At times, it pisses me off that I didn't do what I was supposed to do before you stepped in. As fucked up as I was, Rayshon, and maybe you have forgotten, but you started fucking *my wife* before she and I were divorced. I made a huge open lane for you to drive right in and take *my wife,* and if you continue on the path that you are on and don't stop and start listening to her about how she feels, you are going to open the same lane."

"So, you think you are going to swoop in and be there for Leila when I fuck up?" Ray said. He moved closer to Devon's desk. "The difference is, Devon, that your marriage was already over when Leila and I got together. You didn't go into good-guy mode until after you knew Leila wasn't going to sit around waiting on your ass anymore. Whatever your intentions are or whatever thoughts that you have in your head that my marriage is going to end up like yours, get them out of your damn head because my wife and I are fine. And if I catch your arms around my wife or your hands on her ever again, so help me—"

Devon's phone buzzed, and he answered it. Ray turned to walk away.

Devon put his call on hold. "Are you done?" he asked Ray. Ray turned back to him. "Because I will assure you that you can't threaten me or forbid me to see Leila. She is my daughter's mother, and one day, I may hug her or rub her shoulders if that's what she needs. So please, let's just be real. You can't shut down my relationship with her."

Ray left Devon's office, furious. He knew that he could not stop Leila from ever talking to Devon again because he was Deja's dad. He knew that Devon had never gotten over Leila, but he hadn't thought Devon would be foolish enough to try to pursue a relationship with her. Now that he had confirmation that he was still the same ol' Devon, he headed home to talk to Leila.

When he walked into their house, he was surprised to see a room full of women with babies in their arms.

"Ray, babe, what are you doing home?" Leila asked when she noticed him.

"I came home to talk to you. What's going on?" he asked.

Leila stood and walked over to him while the other women in the room whispered to each other. He heard one of them say how fine she thought he was and figured they were all talking about him.

"Come, follow me, and I'll explain," Leila said, leading him into another room.

"Babe, what's with the room full of ladies and babies?" he asked, confused.

"Well, I decided to host a group for women who are having a hard time with staying home when they are used to working," she said and looked away.

"You mean to tell me that women really have a hard time with leaving work to care for their own babies?" he asked in disbelief.

"Well, yeah, some find it hard to cope."

"Unbelievable," he said with a straight face. "I didn't know motherhood was such a task or a settlement. Good God, didn't any of these women think of this before they conceived?" He stopped. This wasn't why he had come home. "Anyway, I stopped by to tell you that I don't want you speaking to Devon at all, understood? Unless it involves DJ, there is no reason you guys should be talking."

"Ray, come on, baby. I told you, there is absolutely nothing between Devon and me. Now, I can't stand here and honestly tell you that we won't discuss things that are not about DJ. Come on now, Ray, be reasonable, honey, and trust me," she said, moving closer to him.

"I do trust you, Leila. I mean, I'm trying to trust you, babe, but I don't trust Devon, okay? I'm being so honest with you, Leila, and I mean this. If you want this marriage to work, you have to make a choice. I will not continue to watch this movie that you and Devon are starring in. It's not cool, and I'm not having it anymore. If you love me, Lei, the way you say you do, giving up this so-called friendship you have with him shouldn't be hard."

"Ray, babe, come on. You know me, babe. You know me, and I told you the other night that I'm yours, and I'm here for you. Please don't make me do this. I don't want Devon, baby. I don't want him, but I need him as my friend. He understands me, he listens to me, and he knows what I'm going through at times when nobody understands me. I need him as a friend."

Rayshon couldn't believe his ears. "What? Are you serious, Leila? What am I to you? I understand you, and I listen to you. I may not agree with everything, but I'm here 110 percent, and what you think you need with Devon is—no—*should* be with me."

"Baby, you know what? You're right, and I'm sorry, Ray. Like I promised you the other night, it's done. I'll share with you all the things that I felt I couldn't. I want to give you the opportunity to really understand me, Ray. I want us to be closer than what we have been lately, babe." She hugged him.

Ray heard her words, but it felt like things were still off, and he didn't know how to remedy that.

"Okay, babe, get back to your group. I'm gonna run up and change and head to the gym." He gave her a deep, passionate kiss. He felt as if that were the last kiss he'd ever give to her, and he didn't want to leave her alone for a second because he knew evil-ass Devon was waiting in the cut, waiting to catch Leila at her most vulnerable state.

He ran up and changed into his sweats and a fitted tank, then went into the family room to say goodbye. All eyes were glued on him.

"I'm gone, babe. I'll see you later for dinner. I promise to be home by seven," he said.

"Seven, babe? Are you sure?" Leila asked.

"Yep, yo' man will be home by seven."

"Okay, babe, I'll see you," she said.

He gave her a quick peck and made his way to the door. Before he went out, he heard the women's comments about his body and how good he looked. He shook his head with a smile and climbed into his vehicle.

Chapter Thirteen

Christa pulled into the parking space next to Devon's car. She was anxious to see what type of surprise he had for her. He had called her earlier that afternoon, telling her that he didn't want to slow things down, and he couldn't wait to see her. He told her that she was right about him feeling as if he owed Leila because he had been a terrible husband, but he stressed to her that he had no romantic feelings for Leila, and he wanted another chance to make it up to her.

She agreed, of course, because she had deep feelings for him, and she genuinely wanted things to work. He calling her that afternoon made her feel confident that this thing between them was going to be just fine.

When she got off the elevator, she took a deep breath before she rang the doorbell to shake off the butterflies in her tummy.

"It's open," she heard him yell, so she turned the doorknob. When she walked in, she saw lit candles everywhere in the room. Dozens of candles—even candles along the floor. She smiled because the warm glow looked beautiful. She breathed in deeply and inhaled the sweetest aroma of food she had smelled in a long time.

"Come on in," Devon said, walking over to greet her. "Dinner is almost ready."

She smiled. "Wow, Devon. This is a pleasant surprise. This is lovely."

He took her hand and led her to the table. "I'm glad that you like it. Now, come and have a seat, and I'll pour you a glass of wine," he said, and she did. "I'll be right back." He grabbed the remote to turn on a little jazz, then went back into the kitchen.

"Do you need any help?"

"Nope. You just relax and let me serve you."

Christa smiled. This gesture of romance wasn't a surprise to her because Devon always did sweet things for her, including sending her flowers. If she had an audition, he'd be sure to send her flowers for good luck, and when he took her out, he took her to fancy places. She enjoyed spending time with him, and she hoped that this would be the night that their relationship got physical beyond a long good night kiss.

"Wow, this looks delicious," she said when Devon put a plate of chicken alfredo with vibrant green broccoli and bright red diced tomatoes in front of her. He set a basket of breadsticks on the table, and even though she never touched bread because it was loaded with carbs, she grabbed a breadstick with a quickness.

They ate and made small talk, and when they finished, Devon told her to have a seat on the sofa with a glass of wine while he cleared the table. He came back and sat next to her, and she lay back in his arms.

"Devon, thank you. Dinner was great, and this feeling right now, being with you, feels so good." She took a sip of her wine and handed him her glass. He put it on the end table beside him.

"It does, doesn't it?" he said, agreeing with her.

"Yes," she said with a smile.

"Christa, I know you think I'm still stuck on Leila, but I'm not. I wanted to do something grand to show you that I'm where I wanna be. I love spending time with you, and you are, like, the most gorgeous woman I've ever laid eyes on," he said. Christa smiled. "What Leila and I had was great in the beginning, and then that quickly faded. I didn't want that to happen with us. I know I took things way too slow, but tonight, I want to take this to another level."

He turned her head to kiss her. He deepened the kiss, and then his hands were massaging her breasts. Then he picked her up from the sofa and took her to his bed. There, he slowly undressed her, and then he undressed. He climbed into bed and reached for her.

"Devon, are you sure it's me you want?" she asked.

"Yes," he said, looking her in the eyes.

She kissed him and climbed on top of him, straddling him, and he grabbed her breasts firmly and went right to left, licking and sucking her nipples, causing a wetness that she couldn't remember having in a long time. She couldn't wait to have him inside her.

"Aaah," she moaned. Devon had skills when it came to pleasuring her nipples. Her pussy ached, but she didn't want to rush him. He continued to please her breasts, and even though it was their first time making love, Christa wanted to please him orally. She broke away from his kisses and began to kiss her way down his chest, making her way to his stomach. She stroked him up and down before taking him inside of her mouth. She slurped and licked on it, intent on giving him the pleasure of his life.

Her pussy was ready. "I want you inside of me, baby," she whispered.

                         ***

"You want it, baby?" Devon moved his hand between Christa's legs. He felt how wet she was, and his dick throbbed harder. He wanted to feel her too. "Hold on," he said, reaching for the condoms.

Christa flipped on her back, and after Devon put on the rubber, he pushed her legs back as far as she could tolerate it and slid down inside of her. It may have been months for her, but he had found a way to get ass when he needed it. He hadn't been ready to go there with Christa yet, because his main reason for hooking up with her was to make Leila jealous. After dating her for two months, though, Leila had announced that she was pregnant, something that he knew would put his mission of getting her back on hold.

He had continued to date Christa and half-grown to like her, but she still wasn't Leila. As beautiful and talented as Christa was, and as good as it felt to be inside her, she still wasn't his Leila. And he hated using her, hoping to get back with Leila.

Christa lay in his arms, and he wished she were Leila. He wondered what his next move would be, how he could get back close to Leila. Since the day in the kitchen, she had been avoiding him and not answering his calls. He had gone by to pick up Deja the day before, and Leila pretended she had somewhere she had to be and rushed off without even looking him in the eye.

"Devon?" Christa whispered.

"Yes?" he answered.

"I love you," she said.

His eyes widened. He had known this was going to come because he and Christa were somehow finally getting closer. He did care about her, maybe not love, but he said it back.

"I love you too," he said, barely above a whisper but loud enough for her to hear him.

She drifted off to sleep, and he lay there, wishing he could go back in time and have a do-over. He would give Leila the world instead of grief if he could turn back the hands of time. He blinked back his tears and kissed Christa on the forehead before he finally went to sleep.

Chapter Fourteen

"Ray, you have a call on line one," Catrice said over the intercom. Ray looked at his watch, and he knew it was Leila. He was late again. He was thirty minutes late, and the night before, he had been more than an hour late. He hated that some of his appointments ran over. He tried to run the gym and still do his clients, and it consumed all of his time. He had so many clients that wanted to continue to work with him, and his time was always taken.

"This is Ray," he said after picking up one of the phones on the floor.

"Babe, you do know what time it is, right?"

"Yes, I know, and I'm trying to wrap it up, Lei. I got behind. I had some equipment over at gym two go down, and I had to meet the service guy over there, and that threw me off, love."

"So, how late will it be tonight?" she asked.

Ray could hear the annoyance in her tone. "I honestly don't know, babe."

"Okay, I'm going to get the kids fed and into bed by myself again, and if I'm not too tired afterward, I'll wait up."

"Aw, babe, don't sound like that. You know I'd rather be home than here. It's just busy as hell, Lei."

"I know, Rayshon, I'll see you later," she said, and they hung up.

***

Leila was disappointed that Ray was going to be late again. She put the baby down, and then her doorbell rang. She wondered who the hell was at her door without calling. She looked out the peephole and saw Christa.

She opened the door. "Ummm, Christa, what's up, and why are you grinning so hard?"

"We did it, we did it, we did it," Christa said, doing a little dance.

"Who is we, and what did y'all do?" Leila asked, walking back toward the kitchen with Christa behind her. Christa put her purse down, grabbed a wineglass, and went to the wine cooler. "Christa, what?" Leila asked, impatient.

Christa filled her glass before she spoke. She took a gulp and then looked Leila in the eyes. "Last night, Devon and I made love," she squealed.

Leila tilted her head. Her first thought was, *What the fuck?* but then she remembered that Devon wasn't her husband anymore. He was Christa's man. "Okay," she said, "and why do I need to know this information?"

"Because, Leila, I have no one else to tell. You know, after Michelle landed her thing with *Vogue,* we stopped talking. Well, she stopped calling me. That bitch! And now you are my closest friend."

"Christa, I told you that I don't want to hear a word about you, Devon, and sex. I'm not comfortable with that."

"But, Leila, I am high right now off Devon, and I gotta tell someone. I'm bursting," she said, walking over to Leila and grabbing her arms.

God, I wanna slap you, Leila thought as she looked at Christa. "Wait, if you have to tell me, I don't want graphics, okay? And I have to get a drink." She went for the wine bottle. After she took three good swallows, she said, "Go ahead."

Christa started beaming and telling her about the candles and the dinner. She skipped the blow-by-blow in the bed and ended with, "He said he loved me."

Leila was glad Christa was gazing at the ceiling and didn't see the look on her face. "Really?"

"Yes, yes, he said it." She clapped her tiny hands together.

"Wow, that's great," Leila said, glad that Christa was too caught up in her bliss to notice that her reaction wasn't a good one. She moved to the steps and called the kids down for dinner. "Well, listen," she said to Christa, "I have to feed my little ones and get them bathed and in bed." She hoped Christa would take the hint to leave.

"Oh, I'm good, I'll just have another glass and chill on the sofa," she said.

Leila didn't argue. After the smoke cleared and the kids were down, she realized it had been two-and-a-half hours since she had spoken to Ray, and Christa was still sitting on her couch. Why she was still there, Leila didn't know, but what she did know was that she didn't want to hear another damn detail about her and Devon.

She didn't understand why she was feeling so cheerless about them. They had been dating for months, and she knew that they would eventually have sex, so she didn't understand why it was bothering her. She didn't want Devon, she had Ray, and he was definitely no second prize. Ray was loving, smart, funny, and successful. And the lovemaking with Rayshon was the epitome of good loving. He treated Leila better than Devon had ever treated her. So she didn't understand why she had these

mixed feelings about Devon being with Christa. She
wanted that jealous, angry feeling to go away, but she
didn't know how to make it stop.

She took a deep breath and walked into the family
room. Christa was on the phone, smiling and blushing.
Leila knew she was talking to Devon, and she rolled her
eyes.

"Christa," she whispered.

Christa held up a finger, signaling for her to hold
on, so she did. She went into the kitchen and started to
clean. She looked at the clock and wondered what was
keeping Ray. She grabbed the cordless and dialed his cell
and got the voicemail. She called the gym, and when the
automatic system picked up, she hung up.

She glanced over at Christa on the sofa, on the phone
cheesing and twirling her hair, talking to her first love.
Then she went to the freezer and snatched it open to
see how many bags of milk she had pumped. After she
counted three days' worth, she grabbed the wine and
poured herself another glass.

Chapter Fifteen

Ray wanted to head home, but Ankwan called him, telling him there was an issue with the system at gym one, and he couldn't get it resolved. Ray tried to walk him through it over the phone, but Ankwan couldn't get it to work, so after he left gym three, he headed over. It took him less than five minutes to do what was needed, and he wondered if Ankwan was really capable of running the facility.

After Ray finished, he walked around and looked at the bathrooms and locker rooms and made sure everything looked the way it should after closing. Everything checked out perfectly, so he figured he'd just have to come and give Ankwan another refresher on the system.

Ray was locking the door when he happened to see a familiar face on the street, pacing back and forth with the phone to her ear. She was yelling, so he walked over.

"Karen," he called out.

When she saw him, she breathed a sigh of relief. "I think I have help. I'll call you back," she said into the phone and hung up. "Ray, oh my God. Thank God. I have a flat. I was on my way to Jay's, and I ran over something, and it just made my tire burst, and I have never changed a tire in my life," she said, frantic.

Ray looked at the tire. "I assume you have a spare?"

"Yes, I've had it forever. I've never had a flat tire," Karen said.

He told her to pop the trunk, and he found a brand-new spare tire under the trunk floor. He took it out and put it on for her.

"Wow, thanks, Ray," Karen said with a grateful smile on her face. "I had no clue where to begin to change a tire, and if I hadn't seen you . . . Thank you so much," she said.

"You're welcome, Karen, but I need to be heading home."

"Aw, come on. At least let me buy you a beer. I mean, Jay's is, like, right up the street," she said.

Ray knew he should say no, but a cold beer sounded nice after changing her tire. He looked at his watch. It was after eleven, so he figured Leila was sleeping anyway. He decided to take Karen up on her offer.

"Okay, but let me run back inside to clean up. And then just one beer, because I've got to head home. It's late enough, and I know Leila is cussing me out."

"How do you deal with that?"

"Deal with what?" he asked.

"The checking in and nagging and not being able to hang and have more than one beer if you wanted to?"

"Well, it's called marriage, Karen. I don't look at it as a negative thing. And if I wanted to have more than one beer, I would. It's just that my wife needs me too. She's home all day with my kids, and I know she needs a break. I'll tell you the truth, I'd rather be with them than hanging out with sweaty-ass clients all day," he said, and she laughed a little.

They went inside the gym, and Ray went to wash his hands and arms, then went to the front and grabbed a fresh T-shirt from the rack. When he pulled the old shirt over his head to change, he caught Karen biting her bottom lip and staring, but he didn't say anything.

***

How she didn't snatch Rayshon up back then was beyond her. She wasn't going to stop until she had him this time. When she initially met him, she thought he was gorgeous. She got his number, and even though her girlfriend, Leslie, advised her not to call him at one a.m., she went against her advice and called him anyway. She had an idea that it may be a one-nighter, but she wanted him and decided to take her chances.

When she arrived, he opened the door looking fine as hell in his basketball shorts and no shirt. They didn't talk much before he had her singing his name. He was such a passionate lover, and Karen hadn't had sex that good in forever. She was hooked from the very first encounter.

The next morning, when he woke her, it was close to noon. He had her clothes neatly folded on a chair and offered her fresh towels to shower with and a toothbrush. She was impressed with the hospitality he showed her, and she was even more impressed when she came out to breakfast. She didn't have a man at the time, and she remembered being on a loser roll. She hadn't met anyone who treated her like a lady in a while.

She was surprised that he not only didn't have her clothes on the porch, but he allowed her to sleep in, take a shower, and he made her breakfast. Before she left, he serviced her body again, followed by a gentle kiss goodbye. She was mesmerized, and all she knew was she wanted him and wanted him to be her man. She went home and sat by the phone the entire day, waiting for him to call, but he never did. After several unanswered calls, she made a courageous attempt to see him and dropped by his loft.

She felt foolish after he checked her at the door, and she had no idea the woman that she met in the hall that day was the one he was interested in and the one she would lose him to. She called him that evening, and she knew it was a brush-off when he told her that he didn't do too much hanging during the week. She had asked him out anyway, and he told her that he'd hook up with her later. She agreed . . . That's just how quickly she became caught up on him.

She called him for another month straight, and he never answered. She texted him several times, and he never replied. After a month of trying to get his attention, she eased up and would text or call him periodically to see if he'd ever reply. Not once did he ever respond. Soon after, his number changed, and he moved out of his loft. She was determined to locate him. She came across the business card that he had given her when they first met and saw a website address on it. She went to the website and learned that he had opened a gym.

She was devastated a couple of days later when she found out he had gotten married. She had fallen in love with Ray after spending just one night with him, and she couldn't shake her feelings for him, no matter who she dated. She tried to move on, but Rayshon always lingered in her mind. Over the years, she had kept an eye on him, waiting for her opportunity to catch Leila slipping and take her man.

She was thrilled when she saw his third location going up across the street from her job. It was the perfect way for her to come back into his life without him being suspicious and without him knowing she had been secretly in love with him for six long years.

When she went in to start her membership, she asked the sales agent if Rayshon would be working at that

location and if he would be taking on any new clients.
When the agent said yes and that he had a few more slots
available, she had taken one.

She counted down the days for the grand opening and
excitedly waited for her first session with him. She didn't
know how he would react to her after all those years, but
she was happy to see he was still the perfect gentleman
she remembered him being. She just had to find a way to
make him see that it had been a mistake for him to get
with Leila when he had a perfect opportunity to be with
her first.

"You ready?" he asked, snapping her back to the present.

She smiled and got up from the leather sofa she was sitting on, and they walked out to her car. She tried to convince him to ride with her, but he insisted he'd follow her, so she just agreed.

When they entered the club, there was a nice crowd. The only table they could find was in a corner toward the back. Karen excused herself to the ladies' room, and Rayshon could tell she freshened up because her lips were glowing from all the newly applied gloss. He smiled a little because he was flattered, but his mind was nowhere near hooking up with her.

The server finally came over and took their drink orders, and since the music was a little loud, he slid his chair a little closer so he could hear what Karen was saying.

By drink number three, he was feeling relaxed and forgot about the time and getting home. He and Karen were having a good time, and she had him laughing.

"Hey, what's up, man?"

Ray looked up and saw Julian. "Hey, Julian. Man, what's going on?" He saw Julian's eyes landed on Karen. "This is a client of mine, Karen. Karen, this is Julian, the owner of this spot."

"Oh, nice to meet you," she said, extending a petite hand.

"Likewise," Julian said.

"So, where's Kennedy?" Ray asked.

"Oh, she's home with the twins tonight." Ray thought about Leila being home with his kids. "How is Leila doing?" Julian asked. "Cher told us that your little girl is beautiful."

"Leila is doing well. I mean, the store closing was an ordeal, but she is doing well. And I won't lie. My Rayven is just as gorgeous as her momma." He and Julian laughed, but Karen didn't. Rayshon could see that she wasn't too happy to be listening to them catch up and talk about their wives and kids.

"Wow, that's great," Julian said. "We should get together sometime. You know, have a cookout or something. Here's my card, man. Hit me up."

Ray took it and went for his wallet to put it away, and Julian left.

"Wow, you guys are like two old married couples," Karen said and took a sip of her drink.

"Yep, we are," Ray agreed. He swallowed the last of his beer. It was time for him to head home.

"You sure you don't want another?" she asked. "I'm buying."

"Nah, I'm good. And I got this." He pulled out his wallet, took out three twenties, and dropped them on the table.

"Hold on, let me finish this, and we can go," Karen said.

"No, don't rush on my account. I just have to head home," he said.

"No, I'll be quick, I promise," she said.

Ray decided to hit the men's room while she finished her drink. When he came out, he ran into Julian. "I'm about to head out, man," he said. He and Julian shook hands.

"Going home, I hope," Julian said. "Not trying to be in yo' business, but wife and kids are a good thing to have."

Ray corrected him quickly. "Naw, man, trust. She is only a client. She works at the hospital across the street from my new location. She had a flat, and I helped, so she offered to buy me a beer."

"Okay, bro, if you say so. But be careful, because when I asked about Leila, the look on her face said more than just a 'client.'"

Ray knew this, but he wasn't going out like that. "Julian, trust me, I'm good."

Julian nodded and left, and Ray went back to the table. Karen was ready to go. They walked out, and he walked her to her car.

"Thanks again, Ray," she said. She reached up to give him a tight hug that he didn't expect.

"You're welcome," he said, giving her a little squeeze. Her body felt nice. It was definitely time to make it home.

"I'll see you . . . what? On Saturday, we have a four o'clock, right?" she asked.

Ray wasn't sure, but he agreed. "Yeah, get home safely."

He opened her door, and she got in. She gave him another smile, and he closed her door and smiled back. He shook his head and headed for his truck. He thought about how sweet she was and wondered for a second what would have happened if he had given her a chance. But when he got into the driver's seat and saw the pictures in his dash of Deja, Li'l Ray, and Rayven, those thoughts vanished.

When he got home, Leila was sleeping, but Rayven was up in her bassinet, looking around and making baby noises.

He picked her up. "Hey, li'l momma," he whispered. Leila was in a deep sleep, and he didn't want to wake her. "What are you doing up, baby girl?" he asked. "You look so much like your mommy."

Her diaper was wet, so he walked down the hall to her nursery to change her. When he was done, he looked in on Deja. She was knocked out and had one leg hanging off the bed. He laughed. He looked in on RJ and found him snoring like a grown-ass man. That tickled Ray, and he realized just how much time he was missing out on because he was rarely home even to put them to bed.

He held little Rayven close and decided he had to truly make some changes in his schedule before he missed everything in his kids' lives. He went back into the master bedroom and played with her until she fell asleep. After that, he put her back in her bassinet and dropped his sweats and T-shirt on the floor by the bed. Then he climbed in bed and snuggled close to his wife. He felt her grab his hand and lock her fingers into his. He drifted off, and they slept that way for the rest of the night.

Chapter Sixteen

By the time Leila got up, the kids were up and fed. She was surprised that no one had woken her.

"Ray, baby, it's after twelve. What are you still doing home? And why didn't you wake me?" She took a seat at the island.

"Because I decided not to go to work today," he said.

She almost fell off her stool. "Come again?" she said in disbelief.

"Yep. This morning, I got up and called Catrice and told her to reschedule my sessions and if she couldn't reschedule, to fit them in with someone who could cover for me, because today I want to take care of my family. You don't have to lift a finger today, Mrs. Johnson, and you can go to the spa, hair salon, shopping, or whatever you want to do because yo' man is here all day," he announced.

Leila got up and went over to him. "Aw, baby, thank you." She hugged him from behind. "As great as all that sounds, I don't want to go anywhere without you. If you are home today, I just wanna be home with you."

Ray turned and kissed her. "Listen, it may not come overnight, but I'm going to work on working less. I'm at the gym . . . or *gyms*, I should say, seven days a week, and I know it's hard on you, baby, so I am going to restructure my schedule and make sure I have two days off where I don't have to cut out on you guys."

Leila smiled. "Baby, that sounds great."

"Now, have a seat, I have some breakfast coming your way."

She looked around. "Where are Deja and Ray?"

"Outside in the backyard," he said.

"Outside? Babe, it's damn near one hundred degrees."

"I know. That's why they have on swimsuits, and they are playing with the water hose. I told them to go crazy."

She got up to look out the window and saw them having a ball playing in the sprinklers.

"Wow, that looks like fun," she said and went back to sit.

"Hell yeah. You know how it was as a kid playing in the water. That's all you lived for," he said, pouring eggs on the hot griddle.

"I know that's real," she said. She grabbed the juice container and was about to pour herself some juice when Deja burst through the door, screaming.

"Daddy Ray, RJ slipped and fell on his arm, and he's hurt," she said.

Ray and Leila raced out to the backyard. Ray picked RJ up, and when he touched his arm, he yelled in pain.

"Leila, get the baby. I think it's broken," he said. He tried to examine it, but RJ was crying and yelling and wouldn't let him touch it.

"DJ, run and get you and Ray a towel," she said and ran up the stairs to her room to dress. She grabbed her sundress that was on her chaise, her phone, and her purse. Rayven was sleeping, so she gently picked her up and then hurried back down. She was in such a panic she didn't bother to take her scarf off or worry about her appearance.

Ray was in the truck with a towel on RJ, and Deja had a towel wrapped around her.

Leila was strapping the baby in when Ray remembered the grill being plugged in with the eggs, so he raced back inside to unplug it.

Once he slammed his door, they headed to the hospital. When they got there, Ray took RJ into the emergency room, and Leila went to park the truck. They admitted him, and as soon as Ray saw Karen, his eyes bulged, but he didn't care. He just wanted someone to examine his son.

"Hey, Ray, what happened?" Karen asked.

"I'm not sure. The kids were out back, and my son fell. I think he broke his arm." He watched Karen try to take his vitals, but RJ was crying and scared. "Come on, RJ," he said, "the nurse is gonna take a look and see if your arm is broken."

"No, no, no. I want my mommy," he cried.

"Come on, son. Mommy is coming, but Karen, I mean the nurse, has to take a look."

"Listen, RJ, I know you want your mommy. We can go get her, but I have to take a look, okay?" Karen said softly. "How about you hold this." She gave him her stethoscope. "I'll let you help me, okay? I'll let you listen to your heart first, and then I'll listen, and then I can take a look at your arm, all right?"

RJ was still crying but not screaming like he was. He let Ray put him on the table, but he didn't let go of his hand.

"No, Daddy," he cried, "stay right here."

"I will, son. I'm not going to leave you," Ray said.

"Now, this is going to be a little cold," Karen told RJ. He nodded, and she listened to his heart and took his temperature. Then she convinced him to let her touch his arm. It was definitely broken. "Okay, Ray, it's broken. The doctor is going to want an x-ray to confirm that it is, and then I'll cast him up. I'm going to go and talk to the doctor about giving him something for the pain. You'll have to talk to him because it will be a s-h-o-t." she said.

"I have to get a shot?" RJ asked, sniffling.

"Yes, baby, but it won't hurt," Karen said tenderly.

"I'm a big boy. I'm not afraid of a shot," he said, sitting up tall. Ray was so proud of him.

"Well, okay, RJ. I'll be back in several minutes, and the doctor will be in." She turned to walk away, but the sound of Rayshon's sexy voice made her stop in her tracks.

"Karen, thanks. And can you please get my wife?"

"Sure," she said. Her stomach pained from the word *wife*. She went to speak with the doctor and then went out to find Leila. She smiled when she saw how awful Leila looked in her oversized sundress and headscarf. *Oh, this is gonna be too easy,* she said to herself with a smile.

Leila's breasts were hanging because she had no time to put on a bra, and the oversized dress she had on was from her pregnancy. Even though she wasn't as big as she appeared, she looked a hot mess, Karen thought.

"Mrs. Johnson," she said.

"Yes?" Leila said nervously. "My son, is he okay?"

"Yes, his arm is broken. The doctor is going to send him up for x-rays, and then he's going to get a cast."

"Can I see him?"

"Yes, but I recommend you continue to wait out here. You may not want to take your baby back there," Karen said.

"Okay, I'll just wait here, but can you please tell him that I love him, and I'm sorry he got hurt. Ooh and tell my husband the same for me, please." Karen nodded, and Leila frowned, looking at her. "Hey, wait. Do I know you? Have we met?"

"No, I don't think so," Karen said, lying. She and Leila had met at the door the day she had shown up at Ray's loft unannounced.

"Okay, I'm sorry. You just look so familiar," Leila said and returned to her seat.

Karen watched Leila sitting with her arm around Deja and holding her baby. She envied the fact that not only did she have Ray, but she had his children. But she wouldn't let that stop her. She knew what she wanted, and Leila looked strong. She would be all right when Ray left her, Karen thought as she made her way back to the ER.

She got back to the exam room with the painkiller just as the doctor was finishing up.

"Go ahead and give this young man something to ease the pain and get him up to x-ray," the doctor said. "Once I see what it looks like in there, we'll get a cast on. After a few weeks, this arm will be good as new."

"All right, RJ, are you ready?" Karen asked.

"Yes," he said. He squeezed his dad's hand tighter while she gave him his shot.

"All done," she announced. "Wait, one more thing," she said. She told RJ to open wide, and she swabbed the inside of his jaw. "Now, we are all done, and we can head up to x-ray to get a look at this arm."

"Thanks, Karen. Did you see my wife?"

"Yeah. She's going to wait in the waiting room 'til we're done."

"She didn't want to come back here?" he asked. He looked confused.

"She did, but the baby. Bringing the baby back here isn't a good idea. People are sick back here."

Ray agreed. "Well, if she wants to trade places, let her know we can because I know my wife, and our kids are her everything."

"She's fine, Ray. I assured her that RJ was fine and in good hands. I'll let her know that we are going up to x-ray, and I suggest you come up too," she said, wanting to be close to him. She was happy that she could be in his presence without the hovering of his wife. No way could she gaze into his eyes the way she wanted to if Leila were in the room.

"Okay," he nodded.

After they got RJ in a cast, he was set to go. Karen gave him a sucker.

"Can I please have one for my sister too?" RJ asked.

"Sure," Karen said and reached into her pocket for another one.

"What do you say?" Ray reminded him.

"Thank you, Nurse Karen," he said with his cute doe eyes.

Karen smiled. "You're welcome, li'l man. You are a brave boy."

"I'm gonna be just like my dad," he said. Ray smiled.

"I bet you are, handsome," Karen said.

"Thanks, Karen, so much. You were great. I appreciate you taking care of my son."

Karen gazed into his eyes. She wanted to reach up, grab his neck, and give him a passionate kiss.

"It was my pleasure, Ray. I'd do anything for you," she said.

"I know, Karen, and thanks again. You ready to go, li'l man?" he asked, turning his attention to his son.

"Yep. I wanna see my mommy," he said.

Karen frowned at his words.

"Yes, I'm sure your mom is anxious to see us. Come on," Ray said. He lifted his son from the examining table and turned to leave.

"Oh, Ray, I almost forgot. Here's his prescription. If you have any questions, feel free to call me, okay?" Karen said, giving him another smile.

"I will. Bye now," he said and rushed out to the waiting room.

"RJ, oh my goodness. My baby has a cast," Leila cried.

Ray put him down and took the baby, and Leila pulled RJ to her and held him so close to her chest.

"Wow, RJ, you gotta cast. That's so cool. Mommy, can I sign it?" Deja asked.

"Yes, baby," Leila said, not letting RJ go.

Chapter Seventeen

"Happy birthday to you . . . Happy birthday to you . . . Happy birthday, dear Christa. Happy birthday to you," everyone sang.

Devon had thrown a surprise birthday party for Christa.

"I need everyone's attention, please," he said, tapping his glass with a butter knife. "I have something to say." The room quieted down and gave him their attention. He saw Rayshon put his arm around Leila. "First, I want to thank everyone for coming out this evening to help celebrate with us. I also want to thank Julian and Kennedy for doing such an amazing job and for dealing with my annoying ass because I wanted everything to be perfect." Several people laughed.

"Don't worry, Mr. Vampelt, you're getting the bill," Kennedy yelled, and everyone laughed again.

"I'm sure I will." Devon smiled. "Well, this is the highlight of the night. Servers are coming around with champagne, so everybody who is legal to drink . . ." he said joking. "Please make sure you get a glass." He paused until everyone had a drink in hand. "Christa, happy birthday, darling," he said, taking her hand. "Now, I must admit when I met this woman, it was not love at first sight." Some of the men booed.

"I know, I know, guys. She is absolutely gorgeous, but I was a little scared to date my ex-wife's best friend, but after the first two dates, I couldn't help it. I wanted to see her again and again and again." he said. "After some time, I grew to love this woman. And tonight is special enough for me to do this." He pulled out a ring. "Christa Ann Montgomery, will you marry me?"

Leila went numb and dropped her glass. Ray looked at her, and she tried to play it cool.

"Shit," she said, looking around for someone to help her with her mess.

"Lei, what's wrong with you?" Ray asked.

"I'm fine," she said and hurried to the bathroom. Just as she opened the door and went in, she heard Christa's loud yes answer. "Breathe, Leila, breathe," she said out loud. "What's wrong with you?" She grabbed a few tissues from the box on the counter and rushed inside a stall. She didn't understand why she was crying. "Breathe. It's okay. *You* don't care about Devon. Y'all have been done for years, and you're madly and deeply in love with Rayshon, so stop this bullshit." She took several more deep breaths and fixed her face, then exited the bathroom, looking around for Ray. Before she could spot him, Christa ran up to her.

"I'm getting married," she screamed. She held out her hand to show Leila the sparkling diamond ring she'd just gotten.

"I know, Christa. That is so wonderful. I'm so happy for you two," Leila said. She sounded fake even to herself. She hoped Christa was too excited to notice.

"You have to be my matron of honor," Christa demanded. "You *have* to be."

Leila shook her head. "Christa, I don't know about that."

"Come on, Lei. Who else can I ask?" she asked with her eyes teary. She squealed and hugged Leila when she said yes. "Thank you, Leila. You are truly my friend. I'm getting married," she yelled again before running off to show off her ring.

Leila continued to search the room for Ray, and her eyes landed on Devon. Their eyes met, and she couldn't stop tears from forming. Devon looked away first. Leila turned and nearly ran into Ray. He looked at her and shook his head, then walked off.

"Shit shit shit." She found a table in the corner by herself and sat down. How was she going to explain this to Ray? She couldn't comprehend the emotions that she was feeling, so how would she explain them to him? After a few minutes, she went looking for him. He was gone.

She went back in and asked the bartender to call her a cab.

"Leila, are you okay?" Cherae asked.

Leila hadn't seen her approach. "Yeah . . . Yeah, I'm fine." She struggled to keep a straight face.

"Are you sure?"

"Yes. I just need a cab so that I can get home."

"A cab? Where's Rayshon?"

"He's gone." The tears Leila had been holding back fell.

"Come on, Leila," Cherae said, taking her by the arm. She found her husband, Cortez, and told him that she needed to get Leila home. He said he'd be fine until she got back. "You wanna talk about it?" she asked when they were on the freeway.

"No," Leila whispered.

"Are you sure?"

"Cherae, I don't know, all right. I don't know why the fuck I'm jealous or even concerned with what's going on in Devon's life. I just didn't see this coming."

"Are you over him, Leila?"

"Of course, I am. I'm in love with Rayshon. He's my husband now, and I love him, okay?"

"Hey, hey, Leila. Relax, honey. I am not Rayshon, and you don't have to convince me, but *something* is unresolved between you and Devon for you to be feeling this way."

"Nothing is unresolved, Cherae. Devon and I were married, and our marriage went to shit because he mentally abused me and cheated on me. He left me pregnant, and then I met Rayshon. He came in and erased my past with Devon."

"See, that's where you're wrong, Leila. Rayshon didn't erase anything, and if you loved Devon at any point in your life, as much as you want to block those feelings, you still have a love for him inside of you."

"Cherae, that is *not* true."

"Leila, if it weren't true, you'd be at that party celebrating his engagement."

Leila turned and stared out the window. When they pulled into her driveway, she was sad to see that Rayshon wasn't there.

"Thank you, Cherae, for the ride and the talk. You're right. I still carry a part of Devon in my heart. We had Deja together, and there was a time that I would do anything for that man. But now, the greatest part of my heart is with Ray. The initial shock of Devon and Christa getting married has worn off. Now, I have to show my husband that I'm in the Johnsons' marriage and over the Vampelt marriage," she smiled.

"It will be all right, Leila, so don't worry."

"I know, Cherae, and thank you again." Leila got out of the car and shut the door. She stood in her driveway until Cher left, and then she went inside.

Tabitha was on the couch with Rayven. "Hey, Mrs. J. How was your evening?" she asked.

"It was good," Leila said, stepping out of her shoes.

"Where's Mr. J?"

"Ummm, he just needed a little air, so he went for a drive." She went over and took her 4-month-old out of Tabitha's arms. "Hey, li'l Rave. How is Momma's pumpkin?" She kissed her daughter's little neck.

"She just ate, and she was trying to fall asleep, but you know Rayven is nosy. As soon as the door chimed, she opened her eyes," Tabitha said, going for her jacket.

"It's fine, Tab, and thank you. I'm so glad to have you back. The summer was crazy without you."

"Well, I'm glad to be back," Tabitha said. She made her way to the door and let herself out.

As soon as the door closed, Leila went for her phone and called Ray. He didn't answer, so she texted him. After ten minutes passed and he had not replied, she began calling him back-to-back. When it went straight to voicemail, she knew he had powered off his phone.

Chapter Eighteen

Ray sat outside of the hospital and contemplated whether he should go in. He knew Karen was working the second shift that week because she mentioned it during their last session. After fifteen minutes of internal debate, he opened the door and went in. He wanted to see if she was done so they could talk. Then he had second thoughts and turned back around, but she saw him before he could make it out the door.

"Ray," Karen called.

He stopped and turned around. "Hey," he said as she approached.

"What's up? What are you doing here?"

"Ummm, are you almost done? Because I really need to talk."

She looked at her watch. "Yeah, I'm off in fifteen minutes. Can you wait?"

"Sure," he said.

When she finally came out, he was leaning back in a chair with a hand over his face.

"Ray," she said softly.

He looked up. "Hey. You're done?"

"Yeah, I'm done. Are you ready to go?"

"Yeah." He got up, and they walked out to his truck.

Karen threw her bag on the backseat, then climbed in. "So, where do you want to go?"

"I don't care," he said.

"Well, I don't live far, and, honestly, when I get off work, I want to shower as quickly as possible. Sometimes, working in the ER has me smelling funny when my shift is over."

"That's fine," he said and cranked the engine.

Karen gave him some quick and easy directions, and they were there in less than five minutes. They got out and went inside, and she offered him a drink before she went to the shower, and he accepted.

She took a while to shower, so he helped himself to another drink when he finished the first one. When she came out, she wore a peach strapless sundress, and she smelled delicious. She went to get herself a drink, then joined him on the couch.

"So, are you ready to talk?" she asked.

When he took the last gulp of his drink, and she offered him a refill, he didn't refuse. She refreshed his drink and sat on the other end of the couch, facing him with her knees up.

"So, my wife is still in love with her ex-husband, and no matter how hard she tries to fake it, I can see right through her," he said.

"How do you know this for sure?" she asked with deep concern in her tone.

"Because a couple of months ago, I saw them damn near kissing in my kitchen, and then tonight, when he proposed to one of our mutual friends that he's been dating for the past year or so, she freaked and ran off to the bathroom as if someone told her she was dying of a terminal illness. And that was *after* she dropped her glass of champagne. It doesn't take a genius to figure it out."

"Okay, so what are you going to do?"

"To be honest, right now, I have no fucking clue. I just know that I'm too angry to even look at her right now. I mean, I feel so stupid because, over the years, I let her convince me that it was a done deal, and she was over him and their marriage. And these two motherfuckers just walk around like they are so fucking innocent, hiding behind their so-called friendship." His eyes watered, and he rubbed his face and took another sip of his drink.

"I'm sorry, Ray," Karen whispered and moved closer to him. "I wish I could make it better for you."

He welcomed her onto his lap. She straddled him and kissed him softly. Then the kiss turned into a more passionate one. He kissed her neck and rubbed her breasts, and her nipples hardened. She leaned back a little, causing her strapless dress to drop underneath her breasts, exposing her dark, erect nipples, and Ray went for them, sucking on them the way he missed sucking on Leila's breast before her milk had come in.

He licked all around her chest, taking in the scent of Very Sexy by Victoria's Secret. She moaned and leaned forward to kiss him, her tongue reentering his mouth. He kissed her hard, trying to ease his pain.

"Come on," she whispered, and he got up and followed her into her bedroom.

They kissed, and she began to pull off his clothes. He didn't stop her. She let her dress drop to the floor, and he admired her toned body and wanted to lick her all over. When she squatted and took his erection into her mouth, he held her head and closed his eyes in pleasure. When he opened them to look down at her, he got a glimpse of his wedding ring and was jolted back to reality. His erection deflated.

"No, stop. Karen, stop, okay? Stop."

She looked up at him with a small frown, and he stepped back, bent over, and grabbed his pants and boxers, then pulled them up.

"Why'd you stop?" she asked.

Ray sat down on the bed. "Because . . . I'm fucking up. I should not have come to your job, and I damn sure should not have come here." He fell back onto her bed. He was angry at himself for what he was doing to Leila and Karen.

"Look, Ray, it's okay. We don't have to."

"I gotta go, Karen." Ray got up to leave.

She stood up and put a hand on his arm. "No, stay. We don't have to do anything."

"No, I got to go. Because if I stay, we might end up doing something, and I can't let that happen. I am sorry for this, and I didn't mean—"

Karen cut him off. "Listen, Ray, it's . . . okay."

He headed for the door with her right behind him. "You're a great woman, Karen, and I'm not trying to fuck with your feelings."

"I know," she said, smiling at him. "I'm your friend, Ray."

He hugged her. "I'll see you," he said and quickly exited.

He got into his truck and hit the steering wheel, wondering how he could have let what just happened to happen. He powered on his phone and heard several alerts back-to-back—all from Leila.

Chapter Nineteen

Leila paced the floor, not knowing what to think. She called Ray back-to-back for two days, and he had refused to talk to her. She didn't want to bring their business to his workplace, but when Tabitha arrived, she was dressed and ready to find him. She went to gym three first and then headed to gym two. No one had seen him. Then she went to gym one, and when he wasn't there, she didn't know what else to do. She sat in her truck and called him back-to-back again, and he still didn't answer.

She took a chance to drive back to gym three. He still wasn't there, so she sat in her truck to wait for him. He had to come to work at some point, she thought. After almost an hour of waiting, she was going to leave, but suddenly, she spotted his truck. Instead of him coming into the gym parking lot, he turned into the hospital entrance. Leila hurried out of her parking stall to see where her husband was going. She pulled up just in time to see him dropping a woman off.

She parked a little ways off to watch him and gasped when she saw the woman lean across the seat and kiss Ray before getting out of the passenger's seat.

Leila pulled up next to him and watched him watch the woman going into the hospital. *He doesn't even know I'm here,* she thought. She opened her door and jumped out.

"What the fuck, Rayshon!" she blasted. "You leave for two days, and you're fucking some nurse?"

The look on Ray's face was of shock at first, but it quickly switched to anger. "Move, Leila. Get back in your truck and head over to Devon's, because it's obvious that's where you wanna be!" he yelled. Then he got out of his truck and walked up to her.

Leila growled. "Ray, I am over and done with fucking Devon, and I'm so tired of trying to prove that shit to you. You leave the house and your fucking family, and I see you kissing some bitch after two days? How long have you been fucking *her?*"

"What? Me fucking her? How about you tell me how long you have been fucking Devon?" he spat back in her face.

"You know what, Rayshon? Fuck you. Fuck your whore and fuck this marriage. I have never, *ever* cheated on yo' ass with Devon or with any man, and I catch you kissing some bitch." She turned to go back to her truck. "I knew that I recognized that bitch. That fucking bitch-ass nurse is Karen that bitch who showed up at your place way back when. I'm not stupid. Fuck you," she snarled. She snatched her truck door open and hopped in.

"I am *not* fucking her," he yelled. He went to Leila's window and tried to talk to her. "Leila, baby, I am not fucking her," he said again.

Leila put her truck in gear and sped off. In her rearview mirror, she saw him run to his truck and try to follow her. She was relieved when the stoplight caught him and separated them. He called her several times, but she hit *ignore* on them. With tears streaming down her face, she called Devon.

He picked up on the second ring. "Hey, Lei."

She was sobbing. "He left me, Devon. He's gone, and he has another woman."

"Hold on, Leila. Calm down and say it slow. *What's* going on?"

"Rayshon left, and then I caught him with another woman," she cried.

"Are you serious?"

"Yes, Devon, I'm fucking serious. I saw him."

"Leila, meet me at my house. I'm on my way."

She hung up and headed toward his condo. She was trembling and couldn't stop crying. All she could think of was seeing Ray and Karen kissing. It hurt her to the core.

When she got to Devon's, he wasn't there yet. She got his spare key out of her glove box and let herself in. She went straight to his wet bar and poured herself a vodka on the rocks, straight. She sat on the sofa and waited. Her hands wouldn't stop shaking, and some of her drink sloshed out of the glass. A few moments later, she heard him coming in the door.

As soon as he walked in, she raced into his arms. "Devon, I don't know what to do," she cried.

He led her over to the sofa and held her and let her cry. When she caught her breath, she unloaded on him.

"And how could you, Devon? How could you ask Christa to marry you? How could you?" she asked. She lay her head on his lap and sobbed. Devon just sat there and held her. Finally, she calmed down and stopped crying. "Everything is so messed up. I lost my business and my husband and now you." She sat up. "You left me long before Rayshon, so I should be over this bullshit."

"Leila, I'm sorry. I am *so* sorry for everything that you are going through, and you know I love you. I told you that before I got serious with Christa. I tried desperately to get you back before you married Rayshon. You know I want you back, and if we can get back together, that's what I want. I didn't want to move forward with Christa, babe. But what was I supposed to do? You were with Rayshon, and you told me to let this go—to let us go. And that's what I did, and that's why I proposed to Christa."

"Do you love her?"

"I care for her, I do. But I love you," he said and kissed her.

Leila leaned back and kissed him back and then stopped him. "No, Devon. This is wrong." She stood. "I did love you, Devon, I did. And I'm sorry, but I love Rayshon. What you and I had is over. I want you to move on with Christa and be happy. I don't know why I was upset with you for moving on with your life. I want my marriage, Devon. I want Rayshon." She flopped back down on the sofa.

Devon grabbed her hands. "You just caught him with another woman, Leila. I want to take care of you. I miss you so much."

Leila wished she had never called him. "I know. You have told me this so many times, but I love Ray, Devon, and I want *him* back," she cried.

He pulled her into his arms and held her. "Okay, baby," he said, rubbing her arm. "Shhhh, don't cry, Leila. It's going to be all right." He kissed her on the side of her head.

"Do you have some aspirin? My head is about to explode," she said.

He led her into the master bathroom and gave her two pills and a little cup of water. She swallowed the pills. Then he ran some cool water over a towel for her head and handed it to her.

"Look, you can stay here for a while and get yourself together."

"I just need to lie down until my headache goes away," she said.

"That's fine. You're welcome to lie in bed. The sheets are clean." He laughed a little.

"Thanks," she said.

He hugged her tightly. "I will always be here for you, Leila, no matter what. If you want Rayshon back, I accept that. Just always know where my heart is."

She smiled. "I know, Devon."

She went into the bedroom, took off her shoes, pulled back the comforter, and lay down with the towel on her head.

Devon loosened his tie and realized he had Leila's makeup on his shirt, so he had to change and head back to work. He went into his closet, and when he took off his shirt, his doorbell chimed. He went to go check . . . and it was Rayshon.

"You motherfucker, where is she?" he yelled and pushed his way in. Devon tried to stop him, but Ray quickly moved by him and headed straight to Devon's master bedroom and kicked the door open. "I knew it!" he yelled.

"Wait, Ray, it's not what you think," Devon said when he rushed in behind him. Leila was already moving quickly, trying to get out of Devon's bed.

Ray pushed Devon out of the doorway and stormed out. "No, no, Rayshon. It's not what you think," Leila yelled, chasing after him.

He kept going. He flew out the front door, and Leila chased him into the hall.

Instead of going for the elevator, he snatched the stairwell door open and went through it. She went racing down the steps behind him, barefoot, trying to stop him.

She screamed his name, but he kept going. She finally caught up with him at the lobby doors and grabbed one of his arms.

"Baby, wait," she said, out of breath. "It's not . . . It's not what—"

"I'm done with you, Leila. I don't give a shit about you or Devon, and I'm taking my damn kids," he yelled.

"Ray, please, baby. I swear on my life that nothing happened, and nothing is going on. Baby, please, wait," she begged, still trying to catch her breath.

He snatched away from her. "Stop. Just stop lying to my face. Cut the bullshit, Leila. I'm so tired of your bullshit and this bullshit with Devon."

She stood in front of him, trying to block the door. "Ray, I know you are, baby, and I'm sorry for hurting you over and over again. But please, believe me. Nothing happened."

Ray's jaws tightened, and his temples flared. "Leila, move," he said.

Leila shook her head, crying. "Rayshon, please," she begged again.

"Move out of my way," he repeated.

"Baby, I love you," she said.

He looked away from her. "Fine," he said and walked away, going to the other set of doors. He walked out, leaving her there, sobbing. Devon came out of the elevators and approached her with an outstretched hand. She took his hand, and they went back up to his unit.

Chapter Twenty

"It's going to be okay," Christa said, rubbing Leila's back.

Leila was tired of hearing it was going to be all right. "No, it isn't, Christa." She dried her tears with the baby's cloth diaper. "Everybody keeps telling me that it's going to be all right, but somehow, I don't believe that."

"Leila, Rayshon will come around. He's just upset."

"Upset with me over nothing. He's the one having an affair, and then he leaves me because he thinks that I'm sleeping with Devon. After all these years, all this time, he thinks I would go back to Devon?"

"Well, I'm going to be honest. There were times when I felt that way, times when I felt that something more was going on between you two. You have to see it from his side."

"I have, Christa, and the fact of the matter is *nothing* happened. I have never cheated on my husband with Devon. I admit that Devon and I have been closer, but we have not slept together since I have been with Rayshon."

"I believe you, Leila, but I know for a fact that Devon still loves you."

"No, he doesn't, Christa. He's marrying you," Leila said.

Christa looked her in the face. "Because he can't have you." She stood up.

"No, Christa—"

Christa cut her off. "Yes, and you know it's true."

"If you feel that way, why are you marrying him?"

"Because I love him, and I know he loves me. Devon is a wonderful man, and he treats me better than any man that I've ever been with. But you were his first love, Leila. Just because y'all didn't work out doesn't mean that he has gotten over you. Some people never get over their first love." She smiled. "I have accepted that I'm not Devon's first love, but action speaks louder than words. If Devon doesn't love me, he's doing a horrible job faking it, because he makes me happy."

"Christa, I love Devon, but I don't want him back. Even though it has taken me a while to settle with the idea of you two being together, I have accepted it, and I wish you guys the best." They hugged. "I just want my man back, Christa. It's been two weeks, and I miss him. The kids miss him. I'm so scared that he's going to fall in love with her, and then I will lose him for good."

"Give him some time, Leila. I'll talk to him. And you should pay Nurse Karen a visit."

"For what? To look like a fool? She's fucking my husband, and I'm not going to run up on *her* because *Ray* is doing me wrong."

"Well, she's a willing participant in his affair, and to me, that means a beat-down." Christa put her fists up, and Leila laughed.

"You are definitely cheering me up right now," Leila said. She went into the kitchen, grabbed two glasses, and poured them both a glass of Merlot. Then she came back and handed one to Christa.

"Thanks," Christa said and took a sip. "Lei, I know the timing is bad, and you are in a not-so-good mood, but we need to talk about the wedding."

Leila nodded. "Okay, did you guys set a date?"

"Yep. We decided on January seventh."

Leila almost spit out her wine. "January? Why January? That's only two-and-a-half months away." She picked up her phone and went to her calendar.

"Well, that was my dad's birthday. He died several years ago, and I just want to do it on his birthday. And it's a Sunday, so that's the day."

"Okay, even though January is damn near the coldest month in Chicago."

"I know, but people will come. Plus, it's going to be an evening event with dinner and dancing. I want it to be elegant." Christa smiled and held up her glass.

"Well, okay. What the bride wants is what the bride gets."

They tapped glasses and finished off the bottle of wine, talking about the wedding.

Christa left, and Leila felt lonely once more. She picked up her cell phone and tried calling her husband again. Again, he didn't answer. She left him a voicemail telling him how much she missed him and how badly she wanted him to come home, then showered and tucked her kids in for the night. She went to her room and got in bed and prayed to God, asking Him to help her and to bring Rayshon home to her. She asked Him to help her to forgive her husband for leaving her and for his affair with Karen. After that, she pulled the covers up but couldn't sleep.

She turned to Ray's side of the bed and grabbed his pillow. It still smelled like him. She had avoided washing her sheets because she didn't want to wash away his scent. She knew it wasn't going to make a difference, but she grabbed her phone and texted him. All she could think to say was *I love you.*

Chapter Twenty-one

"Ray, wake up," Mario said and tapped him on the arm when he came in that afternoon from work.

Ray opened his eyes and sat up. "What's up?"

"Here." Mario handed him a beer. "Look, dawg, we need to talk."

"What's up?" Ray asked again.

"What are you going to do?"

"What do you mean?"

"Exactly what I said, man. What are you going to do? It's been six weeks. You gon' have to come up with something because you can't keep sleeping on our sofa, man. The more you irritate Linda, the less ass I get. And, dawg, my woman is not happy with yo' ass snoring on the sofa."

Ray rubbed a hand over his head. "Okay, I'll get a room."

"How about carry yo' ass home?"

"What? Hell no. My marriage was a charade, and it's over. Leila and Devon can have each other."

"Ummm, again, Leila and Devon are *not* together. We got an invitation to their wedding. Christa has told you, Leila has told you, and Devon has told you that nothing happened."

"And I have told you that is bullshit!" Ray yelled.

"You honestly believe in your heart that Leila would do that shit to you?"

"Mario, I am *not* going to keep telling you over and over again what I saw. I watched them carry on too many times, and I know I didn't imagine my wife in Devon's bed."

"Ray, maybe it was innocent."

"Mario, please."

Mario held up his hands in a gesture of surrender. "Okay, Ray. If that's what it is, it's what it is. If you are not going home for her, go see your damn kids. But you know you miss your wife."

"I can't right now. I will admit that I miss my wife, Mario, but I'm no longer in the mood to play second fiddle to Devon. That's *not* going to happen." He took a swallow of his beer.

"Well, when are you gonna go see your kids, then? When RJ is 10, and Rave is 6? It's been six damn weeks, and I know you miss yo' kids. I know you wanna see them."

"I do, but I don't want to see her."

"Ray, get over yo' fucking self and start acting like you got some damn sense. You are going to have to face Leila sooner or later. You need to stop punishing your damn kids and go see them," Mario ordered.

Ray knew he was right. He got up and went for his phone to call Leila.

"Finally," she barked when she answered the phone.

"I didn't call to talk to you about us, Leila, so please don't attempt to discuss us. I just want to know how my kids are."

"How do you think they are, Rayshon? You have been gone for what . . . six damn weeks now. RJ cries every damn night for you. Thank God Rayven is too young to realize that her daddy is M-I-fucking-A," Leila yelled. "I've called and texted you a hundred times a day, and then out of the blue, you finally call like you're so concerned about our kids."

"I am concerned about *my* kids, and I know I was wrong for not responding, Lei. If you want to cuss me out for me not coming around for the kids, go ahead. I just couldn't handle seeing you, but I wanna see my kids. Can I come by to see them?"

"Yes. You don't have to ask me if you can see our damn kids, Rayshon. You can see the kids whenever you want."

"Well, I'll be by soon," he said.

Leila turned off the stove and ran upstairs to find something decent to put on. She scrambled for her makeup bag and fixed her face and hair. Ray may not want to talk to her, but she wanted to look good and wanted him to miss her.

When he arrived, she was fixing the kids' plates so they could eat. She almost dropped the plates on the floor when he walked in. He had grown a full beard and mustache, and they looked so handsome on him. She was so happy to see him.

"Ray," she said, gazing at him. She wanted to hug him so badly, but she was scared to move in his direction.

He smiled. "Hey, Lei."

"Hey." Her eyes welled up with tears. "I missed you," she confessed.

He looked away and rubbed his head. "Where're the kids?"

"Deja and Ray are upstairs, and Rayven is over there in her playpen." She pointed toward the family room.

Ray walked past her and went for the baby. "Hey, baby girl," he said. He picked her up and held her tightly, planting kisses on her chubby cheeks. "You are so big. You've gotten so big, momma. How is Daddy's little girl?" Rayven grinned up at him. "Oh, you are so beautiful. Look how big you've gotten," he said, holding her up in the air. "Leila, she is so fat. RJ wasn't nearly this juicy. And her ears . . . You got her ears pierced. You are so pretty," he said to the baby.

"Yeah, I got them done several weeks ago," Leila said.

While Ray continued to fawn over the baby, Deja and RJ came downstairs. When they saw him, they yelled and ran to him.

"Daddy, you're home!" RJ leaped onto Ray, who had to grab him with his free arm to keep from being knocked over. Leila came over and took the baby, then retreated to a safe distance.

"Daddy Ray, where have you been?" Deja put her hands on her little hips. "I've been calling yo' cell phone."

"I've been at Uncle Mario's. I missed y'all so much," he said, giving them both kisses and hugs.

"Why you not coming home to our house, Daddy?" RJ asked.

"Because your mom and I have some issues that we need to work out, and it's just better for me to be at Uncle Mario's."

"But you can't work out issues if you are not here to work them out," Deja countered.

"Well, I suppose you're right, Miss Smarty-Pants, but this issue just needed us to have time apart."

"So how much more time apart do you need? Mommy cries every day because you're not here," Deja said.

"Yes, every day," RJ said.

Leila lowered her head. She didn't expect the kids to disclose that information to him. She avoided eye contact with Ray, but she could feel his eyes on her, although he continued his chitchat with the kids.

"Well," Ray said, "I don't know. Daddy just needs a little more time to figure out some stuff."

"Please hurry, because we want you to stay here with us—not at Uncle Mario's," RJ said.

Leila hated to hear her kids ask him what she had been begging him to do for the last six weeks—to come home.

"Come on, Daddy, and sit by me. It's dinnertime," RJ said, grabbing Ray's hand.

"Daddy's not too hungry—"

"Please?" RJ begged.

Giving in, Ray went and sat at the table. Leila fixed their plates in silence. Deja and Li'l Ray talked Ray's ears off during dinner, and Leila ate quietly with her head down, trying not to look at him. After they finished eating, they all helped clear the table. Ray and the kids played around in the family room for a while, and then he took them up to get ready for bed.

RJ cried and begged his dad not to leave, and Ray finally promised he'd stay. He stayed in RJ's room until he fell asleep and then went in to say good night to Deja.

"Good night, Daddy Ray," she said.

He kissed her on the head. "Good night, baby," he said.

"Mom really misses you, Daddy Ray. Don't you miss her?"

"Yes, baby, I miss your momma every day." He felt terrible for the kids because they were too young to understand.

"Then why did you stay away from us so long? My daddy said that you left because you think that he and my momma want to get married again, but that's not true because my daddy is going to marry Miss Christa, and then I am going to have two moms and two dads," she said and smiled.

"I know your dad is going to marry Christa. That's not why I left, Deja."

"Then why?"

"It's too much to explain, little momma, and you are too young."

"Try me. I'm almost 8," she said.

Ray laughed. "And 'almost 8' is *still* too young." He kissed her forehead again. "Now, good night."

She pulled up her covers, and he tucked her in. He turned off the lights and then turned on her night-light.

"I don't need my night-light anymore," she said proudly.

"Oh, okay," he said and turned it off.

He took a deep breath and went back downstairs to the family room.

"Are they sleeping?" Leila asked, holding Rayven and giving her a bottle. Ray could see her little eyelids struggling to stay open, so he knew she was on her way to sleep.

"Yeah, RJ is," he said. "He made me promise that I wouldn't leave tonight, so if it's cool, I'm gonna crash on the sofa."

"It would be cooler if you crashed in our bed." Leila locked eyes with him.

"Leila, I told you that I came home for my kids. You and I are not an option right now." He opened the refrigerator and grabbed a beer.

"When will you and I be an option, Rayshon?" she asked. Her tone was sharp. "When you are done fucking Nurse Karen?"

"Regardless of what you think, Leila, I am *not* fucking Karen," he said.

She clicked her tongue. "Please."

"I'm not," he said. He hadn't had sex with her at all. He had gone out with her a few times, but he wasn't sleeping with her.

"Whatever. Just admit it. I saw you kissing her." She rolled her eyes.

"Why don't you admit that you were fucking Devon?" he fired back at her.

"Because I wasn't," she yelled. The baby jumped in her arms. Leila looked down at her, and she relaxed.

"I saw you in his bed," he said.

Leila lowered her voice. "I had a banging headache, so I took two aspirins and lay down in his bed to rest with a freaking towel on my forehead, Rayshon. Devon was heading back to work, and he told me I could stay there for a while if I needed to, and then you showed up.

"I was in his bed fully dressed, not naked, nursing a fucking headache that I had after witnessing my fucking husband kissing Nurse Karen goodbye." She shook her head and got up from the sofa. "I'll talk to you after I put Rayven down."

Ray stopped her. "No, let me take her up."

Leila handed her to him, and he took her up to her room. He took his time coming back down because he didn't want to talk. When he got back downstairs, Leila was lying on the couch.

She sat up when he approached. "Are you ready to talk about it?"

"No, I don't want to talk." He sat on the other end of the couch, and they both sat in silence.

"Can you just answer one question for me, please?" she asked.

He looked at her and didn't answer her for a minute. "Yes," he answered softly.

A tear fell down one of her cheeks. "Do you still love me?"

He could see the desperation in her eyes. "Yes, Leila, I do." He sighed and took the last swig of his beer, put the bottle on the end table, lay his head back, and closed his eyes. A moment later, he felt her ease on his end of the sofa and try to pull his arms around her. He stiffened.

"Please, Rayshon," she begged.

He gave in and held her tightly. He had mixed emotions and didn't know what to do.

"Please come back to me," she whispered.

Ray didn't answer. He just held her. He didn't want to lie, so he didn't say anything. He held her for a while, and then they decided to go to bed. He held her until they drifted off to sleep.

Chapter Twenty-two

"Hey, Ray. How are things?" Karen asked when she approached him.

He looked up from his appointment book to see her standing on the other side of the counter. "Good, I guess. Are you ready to get started?"

"Getting right down to business today, huh?" she joked.

"Yes. I've got a lot on my mind and a busy schedule today," he said and came from behind the counter, leading the way to the equipment and exercise machines.

She followed. She could tell something was weighing him down. After a few minutes into her workout and of him not talking, she asked, "What's wrong?"

"Everything," he said.

"Can you be a little more specific?"

"Well, I went by the house last night to see my kids and . . ." He shrugged. "I don't know. I believe her."

"What? Come on, Ray, you caught them in bed."

"No, I saw *her* in his bed, and she was fully dressed. When I kicked in the door, she had a towel or something that fell when she sat up and when she explained it to me last night, I believed her. Now, I think I wanna give it a chance. Christa and Devon are getting married in a few weeks. Christa seems confident that nothing happened, so now, I actually believe my wife is telling me the truth."

Karen didn't want to hear that. She was trying to be patient and take it slow, but she wanted him. No way was she going to let him go back to Leila. If he did, that meant any chances for the two of them to be together were gone. Things had been going so well. They were getting closer, and after all the dates and late nights he spent with her, she knew he was beginning to like her.

"Well," she said, "I think you should just take a minute and think long and hard about it. You know, be sure. Because if you go back, and she and Devon continue to be close, as you say, you know you are not going to like it."

"I know, and I can't stop them from being friends. As much as I never want to see Devon's face again, he is my oldest daughter's dad, and I can't shut him completely outta our lives. I just have to trust Leila and believe that she'd never cheat on me with him."

Karen's mind raced. This couldn't be happening. "Are you *sure* you can trust her? I mean, trust them? You told me that you caught them kissing," she reminded him.

"I walked in on Devon putting the moves on her. I don't think Leila welcomed it."

"How can you be so sure, Ray?"

"I don't know, Karen. I just know I miss my wife. I miss my kids, and I miss being home with them."

She could hear the frustration in his voice, so she said, "Listen, what are you doing after work?"

"Going by Mario's to get my things, and then I'm going to find a hotel."

"Hotel? That's nonsense, Ray. You can stay at my place."

"Oh no, Karen, that is *definitely* not a good idea. Leila already thinks we're sleeping together."

"You don't have to tell her you're staying at my place," she said. "Plus, my roommate is gone for a week to a medical convention in Tampa. You can use my room, and I'll use hers."

"Karen, I can't. If my wife found out, that wouldn't go over so easily, even if it *is* innocent."

"Look, we're friends. If I were a guy friend, you'd stay, but since I'm a female, it makes it bad?"

"No, it makes it worse because my wife thinks I'm sleeping with you."

"Fine, then, pay for a hotel," she said, giving him a playful shove. "At least let me cook dinner for you tonight. Can you at least come by for some grub? I'll invite Leslie and Trey. We can make some mixed cocktails and have a little fun. You know, just give you a stress break, and then you can go back to your situation with Leila tomorrow." She smiled and nudged his arm.

"Yeah, I'll come by for a meal and to hang for a minute. I do need a stress break," he agreed.

After they finished the workout, they were headed toward the door so that Ray could walk her to her car when Leila walked in with the baby in her arms.

"Hey," Leila said.

"Hey," Rayshon said. There was a slight tremor in his voice. "You remember Karen?"

"Yes. What is she doing here?"

Karen put a hand on one hip. "I'm a client," she said with an edge to her voice.

"Oh, are you?" Leila raised an eyebrow. "I hope you are paying in cash and not in ass."

"Leila!" Ray gasped.

"It's okay, Ray," Karen said. She looked at Leila. "You have a nice day, and, Ray, I'll see you later."

"No, you won't, you tramp!" Leila yelled behind her.

Ray looked at Leila as if she were crazy. "Leila, what the hell was that?"

"Rayshon, that trick is one of your clients? Why didn't you tell me she was a client?"

"Come on, Leila, let's go into my office," he said.

She followed him in, and he shut the door. "Why didn't you tell me that . . . that . . . whore was one of your clients?"

"Because it's no big deal."

"Like hell. I want you to stop being her personal trainer."

"Leila, you know I can't do that. We have a contract."

"Damn the contract, Rayshon. You cannot continue to be her PT after you have fucked her, especially if you and I are planning on working it out."

"Wait. First, for the last time, I didn't sleep with that woman. I went out with her after I moved out, yes. I had kissed her, yes, when I was pissed at you, but that's over. I am not seeing her, nor am I screwing her. She's a client and a friend. And who said we were getting back together?"

"Well, I thought you were considering it. You told me you still love me, Ray, and that has to stand for something. Are you sure you just want to walk away from our marriage?"

"I don't know what I want right now, Leila. I need time to figure it out."

"Ray, please, believe me. I've never slept with Devon while we were married. Nothing happened. The day I caught you with Karen, he kissed me, and I stopped him and told him that he and I were over and will never be again. I told him that I loved you, and I only wanted you, and he understood that. He has moved on, and he's marrying Christa. When you left, Devon and I didn't get together. I don't want to lose you over something that never happened."

"Leila, I believe you. It's just I don't know if I want to be in a marriage with a woman who is not willing to put some distance between her and her ex-husband. I mean, some of the shit Devon and you used to do and how you guys carried on was just too much, and I don't want to go through that again."

"You won't, Rayshon. Please come home. We miss you. The kids miss you, and we need you," she pleaded.

"Just give me a little more time, Leila. I believe that you have never slept with Devon, but some things still need to be ironed out, and I need to make sure that I can handle this so-called friendship that you and Devon have."

Leila didn't say anything right away; she just looked at him. "You know what, Rayshon? Take all the time you need. I won't bother you anymore about us. And if you wanna keep Karen as a client, fine. Do what you want, because Devon was the absolute last man that I will ever beg to stay or be with me. I am woman enough to admit that Devon and I were uncomfortably close, but I've never slept with him, Rayshon, and I don't believe for a damn second that I can say the same about you and Karen," she said and walked out, slamming the door hard as hell.

Chapter Twenty-three

The knock on the door made Karen jump. She had been daydreaming about getting married to Rayshon. She fantasized about him more and more now that they had been hanging out as so-called friends. Her inner voice told her it was fate that Rayshon's marriage became rocky after the two of them reunited. She knew that was a sure sign that they were meant to be together. This nonsense about going back to Leila wasn't going to happen. She was going to use every angle she had to persuade him to reconsider his decision to go back to her.

After almost six years of fantasizing and yearning for him, she wasn't going to miss her opportunity to have him finally. She took her time dressing, making herself as beautiful as she possibly could, putting on the sexiest dress she owned. She would not fail in her mission to take him from Leila. She had her plans all mapped out, and she wasn't going to let him leave without getting him into her bed.

She hurried to answer the door and was happy to see him.

"Hey, Ray. Come on in," she said. He stepped in and took off his coat. "Let me get that for you," she offered. She hung it in the coat closet by the door.

"Thanks, Karen. The food smells good. I hope you can cook," he joked.

"Of course, I can cook. I'm more than just a pretty face, you know," she teased.

"Well, I guess we'll see in a second, huh? Where are Leslie and Trey?" he asked and followed her into the kitchen.

"Well, Leslie ended up working a double at the hospital, but I still have all the ingredients to make us some slamming Long Islands, and I made my five-cheese lasagna," she said and took it out of the oven. "You can sit there, and I'll get our plates."

"Okay, let me hit the bathroom. I wanna wash my hands."

"Sure. You know where it is," she told him.

While he was in the bathroom, she made them two perfect drinks, put a large square of lasagna on their plates, and grabbed the salad from the fridge.

She wanted him so badly she was trembling. She wasn't going to miss this opportunity to have him. When he walked back into the kitchen, she handed him a glass.

"Thanks." He took a sip. "Wow, this is strong," he said but took another sip.

"What's a matter? Can't you handle a Long Island? I only make them strong," she teased and watched him take another sip.

"Oh, I can handle anything, Ms. Karen."

They sat down and ate. "Wow, Karen," he said when they were finished, "that was delicious. And these Long Islands got me feeling good."

Karen took their dishes to the sink and began washing them. "Would you like another one?"

"Yes. Don't mind if I do," he said, standing and walking up behind her. "Thank you, Karen, for being such a good friend. I needed this for real. I had so much on my

mind, but I feel so relaxed now, and it's because of you."
He kissed her neck. "I'm going to head into the living
room. Do you need any help?" He slurred a little.

"Naw, I can handle these dishes. Are you sure you want
another drink?"

"Only if you make it as good as the last one," he said
and went to sit on the sofa. She brought it to him, and he
took a couple of sips. "Damn, girl, it's a li'l warm in here.
Do you mind if I take off my sweater?"

"No, not at all." She watched him pull his sweater over
his head, leaving him wearing a black tank that showed
off his perfectly sculpted shoulders. She smiled. "Damn,
I'm feeling too nice, and you, Karen, are wearing that
dress," he said.

She blushed. "You like?" She stood and twirled.

"Hey, you know you're beautiful." Ray put his half-
empty glass on the coffee table.

He was feeling really nice, a little *too* nice, so he
decided to slow down. He still had to drive. He let his
head fall back onto the couch even though something
was telling him he should go. He felt a little strange.

Karen sat next to him. "So, do you think I'm sexy?"

"Of course."

She blushed.

They started talking about what would have been if
they had stayed together, and Ray finished what was in
his glass. He assured Karen again that it wasn't anything
she had done that had made him choose Leila.

He told her that it was just bad timing. They talked for
what seemed like forever to him, and after a while, he
knew he needed to leave before he was unable to move.

He figured he could sleep in his car if he had to. He had never felt like this before.

"Hey, Karen . . . I'm gon' need to . . . need to . . . chill for a sec. Till I sober up," he slurred. Walking to his car wasn't possible.

He lay back and felt Karen straddle and kiss him. He didn't refuse her. He couldn't. A few moments later, she was helping him off the couch. He staggered, barely able to walk straight, and she led him to her room. He flopped down on her bed and felt her remove his tank before he fell on his back. The room was spinning. In a haze, he wondered how he had gotten this drunk.

"Let me help you with these," Karen said. She sounded far away.

Karen unbuckled Ray's jeans. She removed his shoes and pulled his pants off. He was too far gone to resist. Then she removed his boxers, climbed on top of him, and pushed her tongue into his mouth. He was finally in her bed. She put her tits in his face.

"Kaaarrreeennn, I . . . I . . . I . . . can't—"

"Shhh, don't worry, baby, I got this. Just lie here and let me make you feel good," she said and kissed him again.

She grinded her body on his and kissed her way down to his dick. She rolled her tongue over his head, and even though he was not at full attention she ground her center on him. She moaned, bringing herself to an orgasm and collapsed on top of him with a smile.

He was still sleeping when his phone rang later. Karen picked it up and looked at it. She smiled when she saw it was Leila. It stopped ringing and then began to ring again.

"Ray," she said and shook him. He didn't move. It rang once more, and she resisted the urge to answer it. She held his phone for several moments, and then it rang in her hand again. This time, she answered.

"Hello," she said with a grin.

"Hello?"

"Yes, Leila?" Karen said.

"Karen?" she shrieked.

"Yes, Leila, this is Karen."

"Where is Rayshon?"

"He's asleep." Karen got up and walked out of her bedroom.

"Why are you answering my husband's fucking phone?"

"Because Ray is sleeping. If something is wrong with one of his kids, I can wake him."

"Wake him any-damn-way," Leila spat.

"Is something wrong with one of his kids?"

"None of your damn business. Now, put my damn husband on the phone, trick," Leila snapped.

"Look, he's sleeping peacefully. In the morning, I'll let him know you called," Karen said and hung up.

She held the phone and looked at it as Leila called back at least fifty times and texted just as many times before giving up.

When the calls stopped, she put his phone on the nightstand on his side of the bed. Then she walked around to her side and eased under the covers. She smiled, rested her head on his chest, and drifted off to sleep.

Chapter Twenty-four

The next morning, his ringing phone woke Ray from a deep sleep. By the time he could focus, it stopped. He looked around, trying to figure out where the hell he was. He sat up, realizing he was in Karen's room and wondered how the hell he had gotten there. When he looked down and saw his nakedness, his eyes almost jumped out of his head, and his heart started to race. He remembered coming over for dinner the night before.

"Oh shit . . . Oh shit." In a panic, he looked around for his clothes.

Karen walked in with a tray of food. "Good morning, baby. How did you sleep?" She walked over and kissed him on the chest. "I made you some breakfast," she said and set the tray on the nightstand.

Confused, he said, "Karen, I'm trippin', right?"

"What do you mean?"

"Last night—"

She cut him off. "Last night? Oh, last night was—"

"What?" He hoped he was just naked and that nothing had happened.

"Amazing," she gushed.

Ray wanted to cry. "Okay, wait. I don't remember anything. How many drinks did I have?"

"I don't know. After four, we stopped counting."

His heart raced out of control, and he thought he'd collapse.

"Listen," Karen continued, "I had an amazing time last night, and the answer is yes."

"Yes, what? What was the question?"

"Come on, Ray. Don't tell me you forgot what you asked me." She took a seat on the bed.

She was grinning so hard he decided to sit for what she was about to say. "Yes, Karen. Really, I have no clue what I asked you."

"You asked me if you could have another chance," she announced. "We talked about what we would have had if we would have gotten together, and you said you realized that I should have been the one. You said you were done with Leila, and you were not going to go back to her and be played again. You told me that you wanted to give our thing a try. You went on and on about me being beautiful, and then you asked if I would let you have another chance. After that, we made love."

Ray started to shake. "Whoa, Karen, wait. I'm sorry, but I don't remember any of that."

"Well, what do you want me to say, Rayshon? You told me that you were going to leave Leila." Her eyes teared up. "Why would you say all those things to me if you didn't mean it?" she cried. Ray felt awful. "You had no problem hopping into my bed last night, and now, you come at me with this *I was drunk and don't remember?*"

Ray didn't know what to say. He didn't remember the night before or what he had said.

"Listen, Karen, I'm sorry. I was drunk as hell, and I don't remember. I don't . . . know, but I am sorry, Karen. I'm not sure where my mind was when I said those things."

"Maybe on getting some pussy," she spat and got up.

"Karen, no. Don't say that. You know me better than that. I wouldn't use you or manipulate you for sex."

"And you are going to sit here and look me in my eyes and tell me that you don't remember last night?"

"Yes, I'm telling you the truth. I don't remember. It's like a blur. I think I remember kissing you and us coming to the bed, and you were on top—" He paused, flashes of the previous night coming to him. They were vague but clear enough. "Oh shit, Karen. I'm sorry." He swallowed hard. He remembered them kissing. He remembered sucking her breasts and her kissing him down to his dick. He remembered her tits in his face and images of her riding him. He put a hand over his face. He hadn't meant to sleep with her. "Did we use a condom?" he asked, afraid of the answer.

"No, we were in the moment," she said.

Ray had to blink back tears. All he could think was the worst. "Bathroom," he said. "Where is your bathroom?" he asked as if he never been in her bathroom before. She pointed at a door, and he got up and looked around. "Where are my boxers and my clothes?" She pointed at the chair.

Ray grabbed his boxers and went into the bathroom. He relieved his bladder and looked at his reflection. He wanted to punch the mirror. He turned on the faucet and splashed cold water on his face. Then he rushed over to the toilet and vomited. He didn't know if it was because he was hungover or if it was it from the pure disgust at what he had done.

How was he going to tell Leila he slept with Karen? How was he going to be able to work out his marriage after just having unprotected sex? He grabbed the bottle of mouthwash that sat on her vanity and gargled. He rinsed his mouth and snatched a paper towel from the roll and dried his face and mouth. He didn't want to go back and face Karen, not after what went down. He didn't have any feelings for her. He liked her as a person but not romantically, and now he was put in a position to ditch her again.

He took a deep breath and went back into her room. She was sitting on her bed, looking like she had just lost her best friend.

"Karen—"

She stopped him. "You don't have to say anything, Ray. Just get your stuff and go. I've been down this road with you before, and I know how it's going to play out."

She was right, and he didn't feel good about what he was about to say, but he had to say it anyway.

"Karen, I am so sorry. I didn't mean to hurt you or take advantage of you or use you. What happened last night, I will take full responsibility for my actions, but I can't see you anymore. I have a wife and three kids, and I love them. I want to be with them. You and I can't see each anymore, not even as friends, and I can't be your trainer." He watched tears run down her cheeks, and he felt horrible. He started to dress.

"It's fine, Ray, I get it," she cried. "Oh, last night, after you said all those wonderful things that you say you don't remember, and after we . . ." She paused, wiped away a tear, and continued, "Leila called your phone, and I tried to wake you, but you wouldn't wake up. When she called again, I thought something might be wrong with one of the kids, so I answered."

"You did what?" he yelled, now mad.

"Don't yell at me. I thought you wanted to be with me. I didn't know that you'd wake up today with amnesia!" She stormed out of the room and ran into her bathroom, slamming the door.

Ray finished dressing, and before he went to leave, he tapped on the bathroom door.

"Just go, Rayshon," she yelled through the door. "Get out."

Ray grabbed his phone, went to the closet, got his coat, and then left.

Chapter Twenty-five

When Ray pulled up to his house, he was terrified. How was he going to explain Karen answering his phone? And on top of that, how was he going to tell Leila he slept with her? His hands shook. He was scared that Leila was going to send him packing. She just told him to shut it down with Karen, and he had refused.

When he got to the front door, he asked God to help him out of this one. He went inside. Leila wasn't on the main floor. He went upstairs, and she wasn't there, either. From the scent of Pine-Sol, bleach, and burning candles, he knew she was furious. Every room he looked into was spotless, even little Ray's room, and his room was always a mess. Leila only cleaned like this when she was heated. He knew the only other place she could be was in the basement. When he went down, there she was at the laundry table folding clothes while Rayven slept in her swing.

"Leila, I can explain," he said.

"No need. I'm good," she said.

He wasn't sure, so he opted for the truth. "I was drunk and fell asleep."

"Rayshon, it's okay. Everything is going to be fine. I talked to Walter this morning. You know, my lawyer, the one who handled my divorce with Devon. In a little while, you will be free to be with Karen or whoever. Who cares," she hissed.

"Divorce? You called Walter without discussing this with me? Without giving me a chance to explain?"

"There's nothing to explain. Your whore said it all last night before she hung up in my face."

"Baby, listen," he said nervously. Now that she was talking divorce, no way could he confess to sleeping with Karen. "I went by because she invited me to dinner during our session. I had a few drinks, maybe more than I should have had, and this morning when I woke up, she told me you called. She said she tried to wake me, and when she couldn't, she answered, thinking that something could have been wrong with you or the kids."

"Oh, that's Karen's version? The version she gave you because she didn't want to come off as psycho, crazy, bitch-ass Karen," Leila yelled, and Rayven jumped in her swing.

"Listen, baby, please hear me out, and if you want me to leave after I've said what I have to say, I'll go." Leila stopped what she was doing and leaned back against the laundry table. "I knew that Karen had feelings for me," he said, "and I can be an idiot sometimes, Lei. I always try to be the good guy, and that's what I did with her. After I thought I caught you with Devon, I was angry, and I was hurt, and I really felt that you played me right in my face. I used Karen because she was there. When I talked to her, she listened, and I foolishly played on that. I was wrong.

"After you explained what happened the other night, I believed you, and I told her that. During our session, she asked me to come by for dinner with her and some of her friends. At the time, I thought that it was harmless, and I agreed.

"Then you showed up, saw her with me, and told me not to be her trainer anymore. I didn't realize until after you left how that must have made you feel, and I knew I had to shut it down. I had already made my decision to come home before I went to Karen's. I knew that I had to kill everything with her, because I want you, Leila.

"So I went there, and I intended to tell her after dinner that she and I couldn't hang anymore, and I couldn't be her trainer anymore, and that I wanted my marriage. But I had a few drinks and . . . I don't know. I woke up this morning, and I didn't remember anything. That's it. I told her that we couldn't be friends, and I can't be her trainer.

"I told her that I was going to make my marriage work. She was pissed, and I don't blame her, but I never wanted her, Leila. I was upset and mad and angry at you, and I didn't think. What I did with Karen wasn't smart at all, and I am sorry. I love you, and I wanna come back home and do whatever it takes to make this work." He moved toward her and touched her. "Lei." He lifted her trembling chin. "Can I ask you one thing?"

"Yes," she whispered.

"Do you still love me?"

"Yes, Rayshon. Yes, I do."

He kissed her. He was so relieved that he wanted to sing. "Can I come back home?"

"Did you fuck her?" she asked.

If he said yes, she'd send him packing. "No. Baby, no. I . . . Nothing happened," he insisted.

"Please, Rayshon—"

"No, Lei, baby. No, okay?" He pulled her to him and held her tightly. "Can I please come home?"

"Yes," she said and cried in his arms. "I refuse to let pride and anger keep us apart. And Karen had better be history."

"I promise."

He kissed her deeply and told her he needed to go to Mario's to get his things. As soon as he got in his truck, he called the gym and asked Catrice, one of his clerks, to look up an old doctor client of his named Dr. Vernon. He had been one of Ray's clients for years, but when Ray started opening new locations, he began working with someone else. But he still had a membership with Johnson's Physicals, and Ray knew he would help him out. He called the doctor's office and told him his situation, and Dr. Vernon agreed to see him.

"Look, Charles," he said when he was in the exam room, "I know it was stupid, and I know I should be ashamed of myself, but you know how much I love Leila. Last night was not planned." Ray rubbed his head. "I don't know what took over me. It's like I wasn't myself, you know? Like I saw what was happening, but I didn't have any control. I felt like I wasn't myself, like I was watching myself and couldn't stop myself."

"Well, how many drinks did you have?"

"Shit, Charles, I don't know. She said we had way more than I remember, and I can't understand it. I woke up, and it's like last night was a dream. I can only remember bits and pieces. Shit, Charles, I have never felt that way."

"Well, what did you have besides a few Long Islands?"

"Dinner. She made ummm . . . ummm . . . Damn. Ummm, lasagna. Yeah, lasagna and salad."

"Well, Ray, I feel for you, and I know you wish you could turn back the hands of time, but what's done is done. I'll have Celeste draw some blood and run some tests for STDs. Now, it can be too early to detect, so you should come back in seven days to retest. However, I will give you something just in case, and it won't hurt you. I suggest that you wait about three days before you think about touching Leila and come back in seven so I can make sure you're clear."

Ray didn't know how he was going to pull that off. "Charles, how the hell am I going to do that? Leila and I just got back together today, man. She isn't going to go for that."

"Well, Rayshon, the only other option is to tell Leila the truth. Now, to be honest, the injections will shut down anything, and you should be fine, but I want to make absolutely sure. So, either hold her off or tell her the truth."

"Charles, you know I can't do that. She just told me this morning that she called a lawyer. If I go home with this, my marriage is as good as over. I just looked Leila in her eyes and told her nothing happened."

"Well, you need to come up with something, Ray, because I don't recommend you sleeping with her until the shots kick in."

Ray's eyes burned. He had to go home and face the music. He had to tell Leila the truth. "Okay, I feel you," he said.

"Look, I'll run your tests right away for you as a favor. Your results will be mailed to you, and I will call you only if something shows up. But you still need to come back in seven days for another screening. Those results will be mailed to you as well. If nothing shows up, you won't hear from me."

Ray nodded. "Hey, Charles, can you mail the results to the gym? I don't want this going to the house."

"Sure. Just give Celeste the address where you want them to be mailed. This one is on the house."

"Thanks, Charles," Ray said.

"No problem, man. You've been more than my trainer over the years, and you have given me sound advice to help me keep my marriage, so it's my pleasure. If you have any questions about your test results, holla at me. I wish you and Leila the best," he said and exited the room.

Shortly after, Celeste, his nurse, came in and drew blood, then gave him two injections. He gave her the gym address to send the results to and left the doctor's office. He felt like he was headed to the electric chair.

When he made it home that evening, the house was clean as a whistle, and he smelled food cooking. The kids were happy to see him, and so was Leila. They ate dinner together and put the kids to bed.

Ray was scared to death to tell Leila the truth. Maybe he could just avoid sex for three days. He yawned like he was tired.

"You're tired, baby?" Leila asked. He nodded and yawned again. "Too tired to—" He held his breath. How was he going to get out of this?—"massage my feet?" she asked. He laughed. "What, why are you laughing?" she asked.

"Because I thought you wanted The Big D," he said.

She smiled. "I do, but the curse came today, so she'll be on lock for a few days." Ray almost fell out of his chair. He was so relieved he wanted to leap to the ceiling. Leila winked at him. "But if you want me to hook you up wit' a li'l sumthin' sumthin,' I can."

"Naw, baby. I'll be happy to wait until you're all clear, so we both can feel good," he said, praising God on the inside. He stood and grabbed Leila by the hand and escorted her to the family room, where she sat on the couch. "Don't move," he said and ran upstairs. He double-checked on the kids and then went back down and grabbed two glasses. Next, he went for the bubbly instead of the wine.

"Wow, champagne. You opened our good bottle. What's the occasion?"

"Us. That's the occasion. I want to celebrate us and our family and our marriage. I know it was hard on you earlier this year when you lost your store, then you had Rave, and then our marriage took a turn for the worse. I am sorry for all the heartache and the damn drama and the disappointment I caused you."

Leila smiled. "I'm sorry too, Rayshon. I didn't see what I was doing to you with the entire Devon situation, and I'm truly sorry." She lifted her glass.

Ray lifted his too. "To our marriage," he said.

"To our family," she said, and they clanked their glasses together.

"And one more thing," he said.

"What's that?" she asked.

"Divorce will never be an option in this marriage, Leila. I don't ever want to hear it again. Whatever it is or whatever it may be, we are staying together, and we are going to work it out. I love you that much, and I will never walk out on you and my kids again. I love you that much. Do you love me that much?"

"Yes, I love you that much, baby."

"Then promise right now that divorce is not an option, no matter what."

"I promise," she said and then smiled. "Unless Denzel asks me out," she joked.

He laughed. "Denzel? Leila, you'd leave me for Denzel?" he teased, laughing.

"No, baby. You are my Denzel, Morris, Idris, and Boris all wrapped into one," she said and kissed him.

"Yeah, that's what I thought," he said.

They sat on the sofa all night and polished off the entire bottle of champagne.

Chapter Twenty-six

"It's party time, ladies!" Christa yelled. She was ready to get it in.

All the women cheered and howled. They were at Jay's for her bachelorette party. She had live music and a naughty cake that looked like a penis. Everyone that passed the table wanted to take a picture with it. The ladies were having a good time impatiently waiting for erotic entertainment.

Cher walked in with Katrina, and Christa did a double-take. "Oh my God, look what the cat dragged in," she said.

Leila turned toward the door. "Cherae. And is that who I think it is? I thought you said they hated each other?"

"Well, that's what I thought," Christa said and downed the rest of her drink. She hoped that things wouldn't get crazy because she was sure that Leila still wanted to beat the hell out of Katrina.

"Let me go talk to Cherae and see what the hell is going on," Leila said. She walked over to them. "Katrina," she spat.

"Leila, how are things?" Katrina asked.

Leila glared at her. "Things are fine. Cherae, can I have a word?"

"Kat, go get a drink, and I'll be back in a minute," Cherae said.

Katrina looked at Leila before walking away, and Leila rolled her eyes.

"Cherae, why is she here?" Leila asked, furious. "I told you months ago what went down with her, me, and my husband."

"I know, Leila, I didn't bring her to make waves. Katrina and I are working on our relationship, and I thought it would be nice if you could kinda let go of the past and forgive her."

"She never even apologized."

"Would you have forgiven her if she did?"

"I don't know. Maybe. But that's not the point. Katrina damn near ruined everything for Ray and me, and just seeing her . . . I wanna punch her in the throat."

"Listen, a good friend of mine—you know her—taught me the meaning of forgiveness. It was a gift that God knows I didn't deserve, but she gave it to me anyway. And that's what Katrina gave to me and what I gave back to her. Whether or not I like it, she *is* my sister, and my life is so much better with her than without her. Trust, we had a lot of family issues and craziness behind my mom, but we are working every day to get past the past.

"Now, I'm not defending what Kat did to you and Ray. That was foul, but I have done some foul shit in my day, and I am happy that the people I love gave me another chance."

"Wow, Cherae. You make it sound so easy."

"It is. Follow me." She took Leila by the hand and led her over to Katrina. Cherae nodded at Katrina.

"Look, Leila," Katrina said. "I didn't want to come to this party, but Cher convinced me to come. And even though I fought it, I have to be a woman and say that I'm sorry to your face. I was selfish and mean, and what I did to you and Rayshon was wrong. I am so sorry. I know we will never be friends, and that's not even close to what I want, but I just wanted to look you in the eye and say I'm sorry."

"Thank you, Katrina," Leila said. "I accept your apology. This by no means makes us cool, but from this day forward, I will no longer wanna whip yo' ass," she said, and they laughed. "Now that the apologies are out of the way, there are free shots of tequila, all on my ex-husband's dime, and I ain't scared to put his ass in the poorhouse."

When the party was over, Cher and Katrina stayed behind to help Kennedy and Leila clean up. Christa was wasted, so Devon had picked her up.

"So, how is your new job coming along?" Kennedy asked Katrina.

Katrina smiled. "Oh, it's great. I never knew a job as a PT would land me into physical therapy."

"That's great, Kat," Kennedy said.

"Oh, and tell Kennedy about your new man," Cher said.

"A new man? Do tell," Kennedy said.

Leila shook her head. Women loved to gossip. She was just relieved that Katrina wasn't checking her man anymore.

"Well, his name is Cordell. He's a lab tech, and he is fine as hell. He's smart, sorta on the nerdy side, but he is definitely not a nerd between the sheets." She slapped five with Cherae.

"And, Kennedy, he is fine but nerdy fine. He wears these glasses like Clark Kent," Cher said, laughing a little.

"And when we're alone, he is my Superman," Katrina said. The three of them laughed.

"You are too fast," Kennedy said.

"Leila, what's going on in that head of yours?" Cher asked.

"Nothing, chile. I'm just trying to finish up so I can get home to *my* Superman." They laughed again.

"I heard that," Cher said.

"I feel you, Leila, because Julian and I still act like we're Lois and Clark. Umm, correction, Lois and Superman, because Julian is still lifting all this against the wall," Kennedy said and dropped it like it's hot.

"Ooh, girl, I didn't know you can still drop it that low," Cher teased. "And all that about what you and Julian be doing is TMI."

"That's how she got them twins," Leila joked, and they all laughed.

"You damn right," Kennedy said, and they all slapped five.

The ladies finished up and headed home. Leila was glad to see Rayshon up waiting on her. She told him about her run-in with Katrina, and he didn't believe her when she said that she and Katrina were cool now. It had been years since, and finally, all was forgiven.

Chapter Twenty-seven

Christa and Devon's wedding was lovely. Rayshon was happier to see Devon finally married to Christa than anyone. They were at the reception when his cell phone went off. He looked at it and saw that it was Karen, so he hit *ignore*. Two minutes later, she called again, and he hit *ignore* again. After five attempts, she sent him a text message saying she needed to talk to him urgently. He deleted it.

"Who is that, baby?" Leila asked.

"I didn't recognize the number," he lied.

"Maybe it's someone who got a business card or something from the gym."

"Yeah, maybe." He nodded and put the phone back in his pocket.

"Maybe you should take the call," she suggested.

"Naw," he said, reaching in his pocket again when his phone vibrated. When he read it, he almost passed out. "Maybe I should take this, babe." He got up. "I'll be back in a sec." He rushed to the door.

He looked at the text again.

I'm pregnant, and we need to talk.

Ray thought he would have a heart attack right there on the street. His mind raced, and he couldn't focus. It had been a month since he last saw her, and he could not believe his eyes. He paced, wondering if he should call or text. He began to sweat, although he was outside in the dead of winter with no coat.

"What in the fuck am I gonna do?" he said out loud.

He was scared to go back inside. How was he going to play it cool when Karen had just dropped this on him in a damn text message?

His phone went off again. He thought it was her, but it was Leila asking him if everything was okay. He hurried back inside.

"Is everything all right? Babe? You're sweating."

"Yeah. I ran down to the truck because it looked like the dome light was on," he said, coming up with something quick. "Sure enough, RJ's door wasn't closed all the way."

"Yeah, he isn't strong enough to close the doors good," she said.

She smiled at her husband, and he felt like shit. He should have told her the whole truth from the start, and maybe she would have spared his life. She was going to kill him for real now.

Maybe Karen doesn't want to keep it, he thought, but he knew her, and she was going to want to keep it and want him to be involved. He needed some air.

"Baby, let's dance," Leila said.

They hit the floor, and he tried to carry on the rest of the night as if Karen had never revealed her secret to him. He was so deep in thought on the ride home he didn't hear Leila talking at first.

She tapped his arm. "Ray, babe, where are we going?"

"Huh? What?"

"Where are we going? You passed our street."

"Did I?" He looked up and realized he did.

"Baby, what's wrong? You've been acting weird."

"Nothing, babe. I don't know how I zoned out," he said nervously.

"Well, you need to zone in and get my babies and me home safe," she joked. Ray barely laughed.

When they got home, Tabitha was asleep on the couch, and the baby was in her playpen.

"Tab," Ray whispered and shook her a little. "We're home," he said, and she stretched. "You can stay if you like," he said. She nodded and went right back to sleep.

Leila got the baby to take her up, and Ray went up to make sure Deja and RJ were getting ready for bed. Leila was undressing when he walked in.

"The wedding was nice, wasn't it?"

"Yeah," Ray said, unbuttoning his shirt. "I can't believe y'all pulled it off in so little time."

"'Cause yo' wife got skills," Leila said, putting on her robe.

"You sho' do, baby," he agreed.

His phone buzzed, and his heart started to race. His gut told him it was Karen. He looked at his phone and saw that it was. He lied and said it was Mario. He told Leila that Mario said his car wouldn't start, so he had to head back and help him out. Leila believed him. He changed into some sweats, hopped in his truck, and called Mario.

"Yo', man, what's up?" Mario answered.

"Man, I'm in some serious shit right now. Where are you?"

"Just pulling up to the house."

"Look, I just told Lei you were having car trouble. Tell Linda the same thing and get yo' ass to Jay's ASAP."

"What's going on, Ray?"

"Man, I will tell you when you get there. Just get there now," he said and hung up.

He debated calling Karen, but he decided he'd talk to Mario first. He got to Jay's and was happy to see it was fairly empty. Most people that they associated with had gone to the wedding and reception, so he was almost sure he wouldn't see anyone he knew. He grabbed a seat at the bar and ordered a double Hennessey on the rocks. Tony was back within seconds because the bar only had two other customers. Ray downed his drink and had asked for another when Mario walked in.

Mario took off his coat, threw it over the stool next to Ray, and sat down.

"Ray, man, spill it," he said and waved for Tony. "You look like you're about to shed tears. Are the kids okay? Is something wrong with Lei?"

Ray didn't talk until after Tony served Mario his beer. "She's fucking pregnant."

"Leila? Again, man? That's great. What's the problem?"

"Karen," Ray whispered.

Mario set his beer down on the bar. "Karen? I know you *didn't* just say Karen. What the fuck, Ray? You said you were not fucking with that woman. How in the fuck did you get her pregnant, man? What the fuck is wrong with you?"

"Mario, you have no fucking idea how I feel right now. I wasn't fucking Karen, okay? I fooled around with her one night when I first left home, and then I shut it down. About a month ago, right when I went home, I went to her place for dinner. My motive that night was to tell her to kick rocks, but I drank a li'l bit, or let her tell it, a lot of bit, and apparently, I said some shit to her and made some promises to leave Leila and slept with her. I don't remember that shit. All I remember is bits and pieces.

"I told her that I couldn't see her ever again, and I couldn't be her PT anymore, and left. Then I get this shit, right here," he said, showing Mario the text.

"Wait, if you don't remember what went down, how can you be so sure that you guys actually had sex, Ray?"

"Man, because I have these images in my head of kissing her and sucking on her tits and shit and her being on top of me. But I don't remember if the shit was good or busting a nut. I don't remember shit."

"Damn, you got that fucked up?"

"Yes. Shit, man, I don't know. All I know is now I'm fucked. Leila is going to leave me, that's for sure. I stood in my wife's face and led her to believe that I never slept with that woman, and now she's pregnant. I can't deny that I fucked her, man. What the fuck am I going to do?" Ray lowered his head down and rubbed the back of it.

"Confront her, for one. Make that bitch pee on a stick in front of you, and then when that baby comes, get that kid tested."

"About *Leila*. She's going to hate me, Mario. She is never going to trust me again after this."

Mario shook his head. "She is going to be angry, but she is not going to hate you. And Leila is not going to leave you."

Rayshon wished that were true. "I screwed up. I am such an idiot."

"No, you're just too nice," Mario said.

"What do you mean, too nice?"

"You are. You treat the hoes like they're ladies. Women like Karen are hoes, and that ho set out to get you. Yo' ass be being so sweet to bitches like her, and now look where you are."

"Damn, you know me so well," Ray said, rubbing his head again.

"Look, run by Walgreens, grab one of them home pregnancy tests, and go by there and make her take it. If she resists or gives you excuses, her ass is lying. And if she agrees, don't trust her to do it alone. Tell her you wanna watch her piss and see if she gets nervous. Now, if she sits and pisses on that stick in front of you, the next move is to make sure *you're* the daddy. If I were you, I wouldn't say shit to Leila until that li'l bastard is born and after the test."

"Mario—are you fuckin' insane? If I hide her pregnancy from Leila for nine months and that baby is mine, Leila is going to cut off my nuts," Ray said, looking at him like he just missed his ride on the short bus.

"And if you hide her pregnancy and the baby comes and that li'l bastard ain't yours, Leila will never know what happened, nor will she know that you ever fucked around with that bitch," Mario said, and it made sense, but Ray wasn't sure if that was going to work. He'd rather Leila heard it from him than Karen telling her, just to be evil.

"I don't know, Mario. I can tell you I have never been this fucking terrified in my life. What about my kids? How do I sit Deja, RJ, and Rave down and say, you have another little brother or sister because daddy was dicking around on yo' momma?" Ray said and waved for another drink.

"You won't have to sit your kids down and tell them shit. You're thinking too far ahead—Ray, damn, make sure that bitch ain't lying first, and then your next move is making sure you're the damn daddy, and *then* you worry about telling your family. You got that? You don't tell Leila shit until you're absolutely sure that you have fathered another child," he said, and Ray paid for his last drink. He grabbed his coat to leave. Then he ran into the first Walgreens he saw and got a test. He nervously dialed Karen and waited for her to answer.

"Hello," she answered softly.

"It's me. I'm outside. Can I come up?"

"Yeah," she said, and he hit *end*. He got up to her door and knocked. When she opened the door, he walked in, and she had her head down.

"You need to take this," he said and tossed the test onto her coffee table.

"I have the test I took earlier today," she said, but he didn't give a damn about the test she had taken earlier.

"Karen, look, I'm not here to play games with you, and you already know the big fucking picture here. Now, this is *not* a request, okay? In order for me to know that you're pregnant, you and I are going to go into the bathroom, and you're going to piss on this stick in front of me, and if you can't do that, I *will* get a restraining order against you, and if you come within fifty feet of me, I'll have your ass arrested. I am married with three kids, Karen, and I don't need this shit right now," he yelled, and she snatched the test from the table.

"Follow me," she said, and he did. She lifted her little nightgown. She didn't have on any panties. Then she sat on the toilet and ripped open the test. She pulled the cap off with her teeth, pissed on it, replaced the cap, and laid the test on the vanity. Ray nervously stood there. In a matter of seconds, two lines appeared. He waited the full three minutes . . . and there it was . . . a positive result. Ray blinked back his tears, and she stormed out of the bathroom. He came into the living room behind her and had to ask.

"Are you sure it's me?"

"Yea, Rayshon, how can you ask me a question like that?"

"Karen, this is fucking me up right now, and I have so much to lose over this, so, yes, I'm asking, are you *sure* you're carrying my seed? Because if you're not, I am begging you to stop this right now so that I can get back to my life."

"It's yours, Rayshon, and I'm sorry to interrupt your fucking life. Have you stopped to think about how this is an interruption in *my* life? Have you stopped to think about how *I'm* feeling right now?" she asked with her eyes welling with tears. "You are Leila's fucking husband, Rayshon, not my man, so ask me what the fuck am I feeling instead just thinking about yourself."

"Okay, Karen, how do you feel?" he asked and folded his arms.

"I feel alone, and I feel like I fell for the wrong man. I fell in love with you, Rayshon, and as much as I wish I had not, I did. That night when we made this baby, you told me that you cared for me, and you wanted to try something new with me, and then you and I made love—not me, but *us*. Then you claim not to remember anything that happened!" she yelled, and Rayshon felt terrible for her again.

"Karen, I have told you I'm sorry. I can't help that I don't remember what happened, but you know the man I am, and you know I never set out to hurt you. And you know damn well I don't want to hurt my wife. You have always known how much I love Leila, and if I said something out of the side of my neck when I was drunk, then I am so fucking sorry, Karen. I don't know how to go home and tell my wife.

"I know you don't want to hear this, Karen, and by no means am I trying to hurt you, but I am not leaving my wife, and if this breaks up my marriage, there is still no future for us," he said being honest, and she cried louder. He wanted to console her, but he didn't want her to not be clear on what he was saying.

"Karen, please," he said, and he helped her to sit down. "Shhh, don't cry," he said because after all, she didn't get pregnant on her own, but she knew his situation. "Look, I will help you in every way I can, and I will come by and be here for you because it's clear that you want to keep this baby," he said because he knew Karen had no plans to do otherwise. "I just need you to keep your mouth shut until I have a test done," he said, and her head popped up.

"A test, Rayshon? You are asking for a paternity test on our child?" she asked like he was unreasonable.

"Karen, you know I have to ask to be sure. You and I shared one night, and if I break my wife's heart over my infidelity, trust and believe I have to be 110 percent sure," he said.

"That's fine, Ray, because I know this baby is yours, so if you want a test, you can have one," she said, looking at him teary-eyed.

"Can you please not tell anyone, Karen? I'm begging you," he said, hoping she'd agree.

"I won't tell anyone," she whispered, agreeing. "I love you, Ray, and I'd never intentionally do anything to hurt you. You gotta know that," she cried.

"I know that, Karen, and thank you. I know that is a lot to ask of you, but I will be here as much as I can, okay?" he said, now holding her.

"Okay," she whispered and nodded. He looked at his watch. It was after eleven. He needed to head home.

"Karen, I have to go now," he said, and, of course, she asked him to stay longer. "Just for a little while, but I have to go soon." She held on to him as if she were a child not wanting to let go of her favorite toy. Ray stayed until after one, and when he got home, Leila and all the kids were in their king-size bed. He took Deja first and kissed her, then RJ, and then kissed him, and last, he put Rayven in her crib.

He stood staring at her little juicy seven-month-old body and wondered if he could love the baby Karen was carrying the same as he loved his own three kids. He fell in love with Deja at the same time he fell in love with Leila. Li'l Ray and Rayven were conceived in love, and the baby with Karen was a one-night drunken mess.

Ray tried not to cry, but he looked at Rayven and wept because his actions would affect his entire family, and Ray wondered how he was going to be able to hide such a huge thing like this from his wife.

Chapter Twenty-eight

Six months had passed, and Ray managed to keep Karen's pregnancy a secret from Leila, but it was killing him to keep up the charade. He wanted to say something on a million occasions, but he couldn't let the words exit his mouth. He would stand there wanting to say it, but he couldn't bring himself to utter the words, "*Leila, Karen is pregnant with my child.*"

Rayshon was stressed to the max because, for six months, he juggled two homes. He was at Karen's side more than he wanted to be. She called on him for everything, and he lied over and over again to Leila, trying to keep his baby affair a secret. He and Karen got along great, and at times, he felt close to her, but he still had a hell of a time being happy about the baby because he didn't want to get all wrapped up and then find out that he was not the father. Just the fact that he knew he lay with Karen was the reason he stood in and did what she needed in case the baby in her womb was his.

He spent hundreds on all the things that Karen wanted for the baby because, just like his other kids had the best of everything, he wanted his baby with Karen to have the same. She still was working her shifts at the hospital, but she was on light duty. And even though she was on light duty, that didn't stop her feet from aching, so he sat there rubbing her feet because she was seven months' pregnant, and her stomach was larger than life. Since Karen was petite, all her baby weight was in her stomach, and at seven months, it looked as if it were stretched to the max. From the back, you couldn't even tell she was carrying, but if she turned to the side, all you saw was belly.

"Karen, you know you won't get to talk to me for a few days because I'm taking the family out of town."

"A few days means how many days?"

"A week. We leave for Disney Wednesday and won't be back until the following Wednesday," he said, and she held her stomach.

"Well, I hope my son gets to go to Disney."

"My son will see Disney, Karen. He will get just as much as my other three kids get," he said, and a bright smile lit up her face. He wondered what he said to spark that.

"Why are you smiling like that?" he asked.

"Because that is the first time you've ever referred to our baby as your son," she said, and he realized she was right. He barely even touched her stomach the entire pregnancy. He'd only touch it if she wanted him to feel the baby move or kick, and then he'd pulled back quickly. He didn't want to be connected until he knew for sure. He was only doing what Karen wanted—mainly to keep her mouth shut.

"Karen, if this is my son, I will take care of him, and he won't get any less than my kids get, but I just have to be sure," he said, and her eyes watered.

"Well, Ray, he is yours, and I will be so relieved when he gets here so that you can get your test, and then we can move on and act like a normal family," she said. However, he had no idea what "normal" would be. If this baby were his, his life would be nowhere near normal, he thought to himself. "Come and let me show you something," she said, struggling to get up from the sofa, so he helped her. He followed her down the hall to what used to be her roommate's room, then opened the door to a beautiful nursery.

"Wow," Ray said, seeing where all his money went. Karen wanted nothing but the best for her baby, and Ray spared no cost because he did the same for Deja, RJ, and Rayven.

"Do you like it?" she asked, holding her belly.

"Yeah, this is nice. Fit for my son," he said, and she smiled. "Look, I gotta go. Leila is expecting me," he said, and her smile faded.

"Really?" she said, looking at him with disgust.

"Yes, really. I can't do this with you tonight, Karen."

"Do what? Stay with me a little while longer? Every damn thing is about what Leila wants and what Leila needs, and 'I have to do this because of Leila.' I get tired of hearing that shit," she yelled.

It was time to set her straight again.

"Listen, Karen, Leila is my wife. You knew that before you hooked up with me, before you laid your ass down with me, and before you got pregnant, okay? You came after me, Karen, when you knew I had a wife and three kids, so don't try to play the victim. I told you that I would be here to help you, and that's what I'm doing, and you have to own up to the fact that you went for a married man. I'm sorry, Karen, I don't know what I said the night we made this baby, but if I had been in my right mind, I never would have told you that I was leaving my wife and kids for you, and I know for damn sure I would have never cheated on my wife and made a baby with you," he said, and she sobbed.

"Karen, I need you to realize that this baby doesn't change anything. I am *not* leaving Leila, and even if she finds out about this baby and leaves me, there is *no* you and me," he said, and she grabbed her stomach and fell back onto the rocking chair. She cried, but he had to go. He wasn't going to let her throw another hysterical fit that kept him at her place longer than he could stay. He wasn't in the mood for it that night, and he didn't have another lie or excuse in him to tell Leila for his tardiness.

He didn't want to hurt Karen, but she knew from the start that he loved Leila. He walked out, and as soon as she heard the door close, she raced to her phone. She dialed Leila's number and was ready to tell her that Rayshon was the father of her unborn child, but when Leila picked up, she couldn't bring herself to say it.

"Hello," Leila said again, and then Karen hung up. She fell back onto the sofa and wondered what she was going to do. She loved Ray so much she didn't know how she was going to let him go. For more than six years, she had fantasized about him. She had literally followed him around and fantasized about them being the happy couple that he and Leila were. She knew his schedule and daily routine. She even knew where he lived because she followed him home, and after finding out where he lived, she would drive by and sometimes sit outside of his house for hours, just waiting to see if he'd come out.

She followed him to work, the grocery store, to the dry cleaners, and restaurants when he would take Leila out to dinner. She would sit a few tables over and just watch him eat. It got to a point where she would imagine that he was her husband and set the table for two. She'd even sit there and have a conversation with an empty chair. Karen was so extreme about Rayshon. She would do anything to have him.

The night she had the flat tire was a night when she sat outside dolled up, waiting on him to come out. She followed him, not knowing where he'd be going, and she was super happy to follow him to his first gym. When he went inside, she parked a few parking spaces away from the gym but close enough for him to notice her when she came out. She punctured her tire with a butcher knife from her kitchen, and as soon as she saw him come out, she pretended to be on the phone.

She was exhausted with thoughts of trying to make him hers. She rubbed her belly and hoped the baby would be her winning ticket to his heart. She knew once she proved that this was Ray's baby, Leila would leave him for sure, and then they could be a happy family.

Chapter Twenty-nine

Christa was happy and still trying to get settled into Devon's condo and her new life as a married woman. The second bedroom became a closet for all of her shoes and clothing, and she promised Devon she'd box up some stuff and put it in the storage space that they had downstairs in their building. After she packed away half of her life, she grabbed the dolly and began to move boxes out of their condo and into the storage space in the basement.

When she opened the door, she was happy to see it was practically empty. Devon didn't have a lot of stuff in there. She began to stack her boxes neatly against the wall, where she came across a box that was labeled D&L Vampelt. Naturally, she stopped what she was doing and moved over to the box. She took a deep breath and opened it . . . and she saw a million memories of Devon and Leila's life and marriage. There were pictures of Devon and Leila when they were children, all the way up to college and then marriage.

She looked through so many prints of Leila and Devon hugged up close together, laughing and smiling. Some were them with their eyes closed, holding each other, and that made Christa sad. She wondered why Devon kept a big box of photos of the two of them. She shuffled through and found more recent pictures of Leila that she wasn't posing for, as if Devon were just snapping random pictures of her. Some were her just talking, smiling, and laughing, but not facing the camera with a pose, and Christa found them disturbing, but what struck her attention was the large manila envelope that had a few pictures of Leila on Christa's wedding day.

She had on the black matron of honor dress, and it looked as if the photographer caught every moment that Leila had at their wedding and reception—photos she never saw in her proof package from the photographer.

She closed the box but first took out the manila envelope. She took a deep breath and tried not to cry, but she sobbed loudly because she realized what she thought she could handle was something she couldn't, and that was her husband still being in love with his ex-wife. Even though she knew she should not have, but she instantly hated Leila and wished she were no longer in her and her husband's life.

When Devon got home, it was late. He walked in to find Christa lying on the couch asleep with the fireplace burning and an empty bottle of Merlot on the coffee table, and he wondered what prompted that.

"Christa, baby—wake up," he said and shook her. "Why are you on the sofa?" he asked.

It took her a moment to wake up, and when she focused on him, she realized why she was upset and had drunk an entire bottle of Merlot.

"I just-I just," she tried to say but began to cry.

"Baby, what's wrong?" he asked, concerned.

"I knew, Devon, I knew. Before I married you, I knew. It was right there in front of my face, and I just ignored it," she cried, and he was confused.

"Chris—baby, what are you talking about?"

"The storage, Devon . . . the damn storage!" she yelled.

"Storage, baby? What do you mean?"

"The box . . . the pictures . . . the memories, the ones you can't let go. Devon, why did you marry me when you knew that you didn't love me?" she said.

"I do love you, Christa—baby, I'm lost," he said, and she reached on the side of the sofa and grabbed the envelope.

"It was our fucking wedding day, Devon, and you had the photographer take pictures of *her!*" she yelled and threw the envelope at him as hard as she could.

He looked at it, and she figured comprehension dawned because he shook his head. "Baby, listen, I can explain these."

"Explain *what*, Devon? How you had him take a million damn pictures of Leila on *our* wedding day, or how you paid an extra fee to have them separated for your own personal crazy-ass use? Tell me, Devon, what is there to explain?"

"Look, Christa, calm down, baby," he said, sitting next to her. Even though she didn't want to, she listened. "These pictures came in the ten dozen of proofs that we had to select from. *You* are the one who asked Leila to be your matron of honor, and the only reason why I have these is that I didn't want you to get upset because you are the one constantly throwing something about Leila in my face. This had nothing to do with me. I didn't ask the photographer to take a dozen of extra pictures of her," he explained.

"Why do you still have them?" she said barely above a whisper.

"Well, I had no intention of keeping them. I was going to give them to Leila and let her see if she wanted any of them. I put them in the picture box. I planned to ask her over to go through the box to see what pictures she wanted because that box has pictures from both of our pasts. Time got away, Christa, and since we've been married, I haven't had the opportunity to ask her over," he said, lying, but he honestly didn't want to hurt Christa. He wasn't over Leila, but he was all in with his marriage to Christa. He knew he and Leila would never be again, and he truly did love Christa and wanted her happy, so he couldn't admit to still harboring feelings for Leila. "And to be honest with you, I forgot that I even had these," he said, tossing them to the side. She didn't believe him.

"Devon, don't lie to me. Are you over Leila?" she asked, turning to him.

"Do you really have to ask?"

"I wish I didn't, but—" she said, and he cut her off.

"Do I make you happy, Christa?"

"Yes," she nodded.

"Do I give you everything you need?"

"Yes," she said and sniffled.

"Do I ever make you feel at any moment that I don't love you?" he asked.

"No," she whimpered.

"Then cut this bullshit out," he said and got up. "Will this make you feel better?" he asked and tossed the envelope into the fire. Christa's eyes bulged in disbelief. "I do what I'm supposed to do in this marriage to keep a smile on your face. If you feel that Leila is an issue, she is *your* issue, so I suggest *you* get over it," he said and walked out of the living room.

She heard him turn on the shower, then looked at the burning envelope and pictures and sobbed again. She knew the truth and the bottom line. Even though Devon was the perfect form of a husband, she could see that his heart was still with Leila, and there was absolutely nothing she could do about it. For the first time in the six months of their new marriage, she slept on the sofa. She later woke up and was surprised that Devon not only didn't come to get her to go to bed, but he left the next morning without saying goodbye.

Chapter Thirty

"Hello," Leila answered.

"Hey, Leila, this is Catrice, and I'm so sorry to bother you," she said. Leila wondered why Catrice was calling her and not Rayshon.

"It's okay, what's wrong?"

"Well, I've been here all morning, and Josh called in, and then Sean hasn't shown up, and I need help."

"Where's Ray?"

"That's the thing. He left maybe about an hour ago. I've tried his phone, but he's not picking up. I go to school on Wednesdays, and no one's here to relieve me. I'm stuck, and I can't miss class, Mrs. Johnson. I just can't miss my classes."

"Oh, no worries, Catrice. I'll be there in twenty minutes. Hang tight," she said and hung up. She told Tabitha she had to head to the gym, and Tabitha was fine with that. She called Ray several times and wondered why he didn't answer. When she got there, she relieved Catrice. Five minutes later, Sean walked in, and when he saw Leila, he started explaining how he had to keep his son, and his prepaid phone was off so that he couldn't call.

Leila didn't fuss. She just told him it was okay, and then she headed to Ray's office. She called him again and wondered why he wasn't answering. She sat at his desk, saw a stack of mail, and went through it. She came across a Mastercard bill and wondered what other expenses he had, so she opened it. She looked at the store names and the items that were purchased. They were all baby stores. She tilted her head in confusion. Rayven was a little over a year now, and Rayshon hadn't walked into the house with one baby item in his hand for quite a while.

She sat there, trying to figure it out, and then her phone rang. It was Ray.

"Hello," Leila said, trying to stay calm.

"Hey, baby, I'm so sorry. I've been busy this morning with back to backs. What's up?" he asked, and Leila was surprised to hear him lie so easily.

"Oh, you've been at the gym all morning?"

"Yea, and I just came into my office and saw I missed your calls, babe. What's up?" he asked.

Leila pushed back from his desk because she had to brace herself for this reality check he was about to give her. "Well, what office are you in because I surely don't see you in *this* office," she said. "And tell me why I just opened a Mastercard bill for over two grand for baby items?" she asked, and at first, Rayshon said nothing. "I know you hear me," she barked.

"Baby, I'm sorry. Stay there. I'm on my way so we can talk," he said, and Leila's heart stopped.

"No! You fucking talk right now, Rayshon. What's going on?"

"Leila, baby . . . I—" he tried to say.

"Oh my God, Rayshon—no . . . no . . . no. It's Karen? Is it Karen?" she yelled.

"Leila, stay put."

"No, I won't," she said and grabbed her purse. She raced out the door and ran to her Armada and jetted across the street. She parked illegally and ran through the ER doors. "Where's Karen? Nurse Karen?" she asked the lady at the desk, and before the lady could reply, Karen walked out of the double doors, and when Leila saw her stomach, she almost fell to the floor. Karen must have realized who she was because she stopped dead in her tracks, but Leila quickly approached her. "Is it—is it Rayshon's?" Leila yelled, and Karen looked at her teary-eyed and nodded.

Leila instantly charged her as if she weren't pregnant. "You bitch! You stank bitch!" Leila yelled. An orderly quickly pulled Leila off her and restrained her. "You home-wrecking bitch!" Leila screamed. "You can't have my husband, you tramp. You ain't taking my husband," she yelled before the orderly pushed her out the doors.

"Ma'am, you have to leave before we call the cops," he said.

"Call the motherfucking cops!" Leila yelled, spitting on him with her words. This was the ultimate pain, and she wanted to kill Karen *and* Rayshon. "If that bitch comes out here, I'm going to fuck her ass up," Leila yelled. The hospital security pulled up, and Leila didn't care. She was beyond angry. She wanted to hurt Rayshon just as much as she wanted to hurt Karen.

"Ma'am, we are going to need you to calm down," one officer said.

"Fuck you!" Leila spat. "Don't fucking touch me. That bitch thinks she can take my fucking husband. She thinks she can just spread her ho-ass legs and get knocked up by my husband. If she comes out here, pregnant or not, I'ma whip her ass!" Leila yelled. The security officer tried to calm her down, but it was no use.

"Look, ma'am, I understand there is a personal issue going on, but if you don't calm down and stop making threats, we will have to restrain you and be forced to call the law," he said. Leila looked at him with her heart racing. Her chest rose up and down like a balloon being inflated and deflated at a rapid speed.

"Are we done?" she asked the security officer as calmly as she could.

"Yes, if you are leaving the premises," he said. Leila didn't answer. She just walked away to her truck. She got in and cranked her engine and forced back the tears that wanted to drop. She was furious, and she knew going home was not an option. She drove to a place that she hadn't been to in years and parked. Then she slowly walked to her mother's resting place, and when she saw the writing on the stone, she fell to her knees.

She cried for more than ten minutes before she could speak. "Here I am, Ma, your one and only child, and I'm in a pickle," she said, then laughed because that is the phrase her mom would always refer to when there was a bad situation.

"I know I haven't visited in a while, not since RJ was two, and now you have a granddaughter named Rayven, but I'm sure you know that already since you're in heaven with God," Leila said and paused. "Truth is, I wish you were here with me to tell me what to do, Ma. Today was the worst day of my life. I mean, I thought I had bad days with Devon, but this one right here is more than I can handle.

"Rayshon has fathered another child with a woman he looked me in my eyes and told me he wasn't sleeping with, Ma, and I fell for it, even though my gut said no. I took him back, and now, this chick Karen is, I don't know . . . Hell, it looks like she's ready to deliver, and he never said a word, Ma, not *one* word. And the sad thing is I still don't want to leave him," she cried.

"I wish you were here, Ma. God, I wish you were here," she said. Suddenly, someone yelled out to her that they were closing in ten minutes, and she nodded.

"I know you adored Devon, Ma, but Devon is not the same man you and I fell in love with, and since you're looking down on us, you should know that Devon has a wife now," she said because she felt a voice on the inside telling her to go to him.

"I can't, Ma. I love Rayshon, and as bad as it looks, I want to stay with him, even if it takes accepting this child. Rayshon may have lied, but I know that man loves me, and I may be a fool, but I love him, Ma, so much, and as bad as I want to punch him in the face right now, I can't walk away," she said and touched her mom's headstone. She brushed away the debris on it and headed back to her truck. She decided to go by Devon's and talk to him before she went home to deal with Rayshon. She loved him and didn't want out, but she needed space to keep from severely hurting him.

Chapter Thirty-one

When Leila arrived at Devon's, she didn't see his car, but she saw Christa's, so she knew someone was home. Even though she really wanted to talk to Devon, she and Christa were friends, so she knew she could confide in her. When she got to the door, she rang the bell, and Christa came to the door looking sad.

"Come on in, Leila. I was on my way out," she said, and Leila saw two suitcases on the living room floor.

"What, you got a modeling gig overseas or something? Those bags look pretty heavy," Leila asked, looking at Christa like she never saw her before. Her face was pale with no makeup, not even mascara, and her curly locks were pulled up in a homemade ponytail.

"No, I'm leaving Devon," she said, and Leila almost passed out.

"What—why? Why are you leaving him, Christa?"

"Because I'm not you," she said with her head down.

"Aw, Christa, come on. You know that Devon and I are no longer, so why are you walking out on him? Devon and I barely even talk anymore. All we have in common is Deja," Leila said.

"Well, Leila, that may be all you have in common with him, but that man loves you. He's madly in love with you, and I can't do this anymore. I can't compete," she cried, and Leila rushed over to her.

"Christa, listen, I know that you think it's about me, but it's not. Devon may have something going on for me, only because we were so close at one point, but I promise you that he loves you, Christa. Please don't leave him, please don't break his heart. Devon married you out of all the women I saw him trying to date. He married you, and that's a grand gesture, Christa, please give him a little credit. Devon is a great man when he wants to be, and from what I see, Christa, he treats you like royalty. In fact, he treats you better than he ever treated me," she said, looking Christa in the eyes.

"Leila, I don't know. I look at him, and he seems happy, but I know he loves you," she said with a little doubt.

"I know that's what you may think, but Devon would have never married you, Christa, if he wasn't ready to move on. I know Devon, and as long as he treats you with love and respect, know that we are not doing anything to hurt you or Rayshon. Please unpack your bags and give him a chance. Devon isn't all bad. Trust me, and even if I were available, chile, please, trust me when I say I don't want yo' man," she said, and they laughed.

"OK, I'll stay," Christa said.

"Girl, that's a relief because what I'm going through right now, Devon would be no good to me if you broke his heart."

"Oh my God, Leila, I'm sorry. What's wrong?"

"Well, Nurse Karen is pregnant with my husband's child," she said and blinked back the tears.

"What? How do you know for sure?"

"Well, after he lied to me, and I saw an invoice for a bunch of baby stores totaling over two grand, I went to the hospital, and there she was as pregnant as day. I mean, her stomach looked as if she were ready to deliver right now," she said. Now, the tears flowed.

"Oh, Leila, what happened?"

"Well, when I asked her if it was Rayshon's, she nodded yes. Then I leaped on her, knocking her to the floor, trying to pound in her face," Leila said, being honest.

"You attacked a pregnant woman?"

"Yes, I foolishly attacked a pregnant woman, Christa, and as wrong as it was for me to do that, it was wrong for them to hide that shit from me," she cried.

"You're right, but, Leila, she didn't get pregnant by herself, and you could have hurt her."

"I know, Christa, and I didn't mean to react the way I did, but when I saw her, I lost it," she said, and Christa grabbed her hand.

"What are you going to do?"

"I have no clue," she said, and then her cell rang. It was Ray, and she knew she had to talk to him.

Chapter Thirty-two

"Where the hell are you?" Ray yelled.

"At Devon's," she said.

"That figures. I knew that would be the first place you'd run to," he said angrily.

"With Christa—not Devon, Rayshon, or should I say, Karen's baby daddy? What do you want?"

"Well, I just left the hospital. Karen and the baby are fine after your attack. She had to get two stitches in her lip," he said, and Leila didn't give a damn. "You could have seriously hurt her, Leila."

"Yeah, well, I don't know how many stitches I'll need to fix my heart," she said and cried.

"I know, Leila, and, baby, I wanted to tell you. Every day I wanted to tell you, but I didn't know how to say it," he expressed.

"It was simple, Ray, just say, 'Baby, that bitch I said I wasn't fucking, I was, and now she is fucking having my baby,'" she spat.

"I have every right to be angry, baby, and you know it wasn't that simple. Come home so that we can talk," he said, and she paused for a moment. She knew he was right, so she agreed.

"I'm on my way," she said and hit the *end* button on the phone quickly. Her heart sank. She wasn't sure if she could go home and face him. She made Christa promise that she wasn't going to leave Devon, and she did.

When she pulled up to the house, she squeezed her steering wheel and asked God for strength. Then she got out. When she walked in, Rayshon was sitting at the table with a bottle of scotch and a glass. She looked at him, but an overwhelming feeling of disgust came over her, and she wanted to slap the piss out of him.

"Please sit," he said. She put her purse and keys down and sat across from him. "Leila, I can't begin to tell you how sorry I am for not telling you. I promise you that every day that I didn't tell you, it was killing me inside. I just wanted to make absolutely sure that the baby was mine before I said anything."

"Ray, I sit here, and I hear the words that you are saying, and you know what? Even though I don't want to believe you, I believe you. I am just so confused about why you didn't feel like you could tell me. I'm your wife, Rayshon, your best friend, and we are more than this. Did you think it would hurt less *after* the baby was born? You kept something so major from me, Rayshon. How could you not tell me?" she asked, looking in his eyes. "I'll admit, I never believed that you never fucked her—that I never believed—but I'm revolted at the fact that you slept with her without protection.

"I just didn't think you were foolish enough to be fucking her without protection, Rayshon. How could you lie with that bitch without protecting yourself, protecting me, and protecting this family? We have to tell our children that they are going to have a sister or a brother, Rayshon. That is what's killing me the most because I accepted your infidelity a long goddamn time ago," she yelled and got up and went for a drink. She grabbed the vodka and made it straight. She downed it and poured another before taking her seat.

"Leila, you are not going to believe me, but I wasn't sleeping with Karen. I swear to you. The morning I came home when I didn't remember shit is the night I supposedly conceived this baby, and, Leila, you know me. I'm not going to lie to you. I didn't remember having sex with her or whether I used a condom. I was so outta my mind, Leila, the next morning, I didn't remember anything. After I came home, I went to see Dr. Vernon, and he checked me out, and I was fine. I just want to get this baby tested because, in my heart, I don't believe it's mine. I have no remembrance of having sex with her. Just some vague memories that I may have dreamt, but, Leila, I swear. I don't want you to leave me over this," he pleaded, and she shot him a look.

"Rayshon, I thought I could handle this, and I thought I could come home and say okay, I'm going to work this out, but listening to you and feeling the way I feel about this entire fucked-up situation . . ." she said, and the tears started to flow. She was angry. She wanted to see the man she was madly in love with. She wanted to identify the Rayshon that eased all of her pain and came to her rescue when Devon tore her down, but all she saw was a lying-ass, deceitful man who couldn't keep his dick in his pants nor wrap it up to protect him and his family. She was done, and what she said next shocked herself. "I want you to leave, and I want a divorce," she said, trembling.

"No, Leila, no. Please don't say that," he pleaded. "I am so fucking sorry for not being honest with you. Please don't," he begged, rushing over and kneeling on the floor in front of her. "Please, baby, please," he begged, but she didn't budge.

"Ray, just get your things and get out," she said and looked away.

"Leila," he cried. She got up, and he followed her up to their room. "No, no, no! I love you more than anything in this world. I love my kids, and I've never wanted her, Leila. I want you and my family," he said, and she turned to him.

"No, you don't. You didn't think of us when you made a baby outside of this marriage, and I can't even look at you right now. I thought this would be easy and that I could handle it, but I can't, and I want you to go," she said, and her hands were trembling. She honestly didn't want him to leave, but she couldn't handle the fact that he made a baby with his mistress. Devon was an ass, but he never came home with the news of impregnating another woman. She felt like fighting him with her fists, even though she knew she'd never win. She just wanted to hurt him. She wanted him to feel an ounce of the pain she felt.

"Leila," he cried.

"Go!" she yelled.

He decided he'd give her some space. He turned and went into the closet, and she went into the bathroom and slammed the door shut. She sat on the side of the tub and began to sob. She never thought she and Ray would ever experience this level of drama. After all the pain and misery she went through with Devon, she never imagined another man would hurt her.

When he tapped on the door, she yelled, "Get out!" She waited until she heard the garage door close before she opened the bathroom door.

Chapter Thirty-three

Ray was sitting at his desk, but he couldn't concentrate. It was close to Karen's due date, and the closer it got, the more unsettled he felt. He tried to be happy, but it was impossible. Every time he looked at Leila, he wanted to shoot himself for what he was putting her through. She barely said two words to him when he came by to see the kids.

He had been on his own for almost three months and missed home, his wife, and kids more than he missed anything in the world.

Karen was a week past her due date, but the doctor said he didn't see any reason to be alarmed yet. Ray was anxious every time his phone rang because he was afraid Karen would be calling, telling him she was in labor. Two nights ago, she called at two in the morning, and after being at the hospital for three hours, the doctor sent her home because it wasn't time.

Ray started to clean off his desk because he had too much going on, and his desk hadn't had a major cleaning in months. He came across an envelope from Dr. Vernon that he never opened. He searched his desk for his letter opener, and his cell phone went off, so he grabbed it and read the message.

My water broke.

Ray froze. He put the letter down and called Leila.

"Hello," Leila answered, and he didn't want to say the words, but he did.

"Karen just texted me. Her water broke," he said nervously.

"Okay, well, this must be it," she said dryly.

"I am sorry," he said.

"Ray, please—" she said and hung up.

Ray grabbed his keys and went to his truck. He felt that he was moving in slow motion. When he reached the hospital, he went inside and asked the lady at the desk what room was Karen in. She told him and pointed toward her room. He walked to her door and took a deep breath before entering.

"Hey, you must be Rayshon," an older version of Karen said.

"Yes," he said, and she reached out and hugged him.

"I'm Katherine, Karen's mom. I've heard so much about you. It's nice to meet you finally," she said, and Ray was caught off guard. He knew her mom would probably come to the hospital, but he didn't want to meet her on those terms.

"Likewise, Mrs. Morgan," he said, and he made his way to the other side of Karen's hospital bed. "How are you feeling?" he asked, and she looked like she was terrified.

"I'm okay, I guess, but the pain is starting to kick in, and these contractions are nothing like I thought," she said.

"Just relax. You'll do fine," Ray said, holding her hand.

"Ray, will you stay for the delivery?" she asked.

"Of course," he said, and she smiled . . . then she frowned because another contraction came on. "I think I made a bad choice, Ray. Can you tell them that I do want that epidural?" she cried, and he went to look for her nurse. The nurse checked her again. Since she was only four centimeters, she put in an order for her to get the epidural.

Ray held her in his arms while they gave her the injection in her back. "Ouch ouch ouch," she moaned, so Ray held her tighter until they were done. Shortly afterward, she was resting, and Ray made small talk with her mom. It was obvious that Karen hadn't told her mom that Ray was married because her conversation was mainly about him and Karen being together. She must have finally noticed Ray's wedding band, and her eyes popped.

"Young man, is that a wedding band on your finger?"

"Yes, ma'am, it is," he said, and the shocked look on her face said it all.

"You mean to tell me that you got involved with my daughter and made a baby, and you're married?" she said appalled. "And you, young lady, what drama do you have brewing this time?"

"Mommy, please—leave Rayshon alone. He's separated, okay? So stop asking him a million and one questions," she said. Her mom stood and rolled her eyes at him.

"Don't think that you're not going to provide for this baby, Mr. Johnson," she said, cutting him the eye, and he just fell back into the recliner and put his hand over his head. He wanted to go out and call Leila, but the doctor walked in.

"Karen, really?" her mom whispered.

"Mother, please, it's not like that, okay? Rayshon is different. I'm fine," she said, and Ray didn't bother to dip in their conversation. He was aware that her mother wasn't proud of their situation. Hell, neither was he.

"You better be fine, chile. You are going to be a mother, and I hope for this baby's sake that you *are* fine."

"Ma, please, okay? I'm in labor, for crying out loud. I don't need this right now," she said. The doctor was trying to talk to her, so her mom backed off.

Several hours later, the doctor came back and checked Karen. She was fully dilated, so the doctor called the nurse in so Karen could prepare to start pushing. She pushed for about thirty minutes, and finally, the baby was out. They wiped him off a little bit and handed him to Karen, and for the first time, Ray felt some emotion. He looked at the boy. He was a beautiful baby. He looked so much like Karen, but Ray couldn't see any of himself in him.

They took him, weighed, and measured him, and they finished cleaning up Karen.

"You did good," he told her because she looked exhausted.

"He is beautiful, Ray," her mom said. She looked like she wanted to say more, but she didn't.

"Thank you," he said, and Karen insisted he go to the nursery with the baby. After he watched them check him out and bath him, they let him hold him. Ray looked down at his tiny little face and his glossy eyes from the solution that the nurse put in them and didn't know what to say.

"Hey, little man. You're finally here, and you are a handsome little man," he said, still trying to see himself in him. RJ and Rayven looked like Leila too, but he could still see himself in them, but he could not see any similarities in this baby. The nurse put him back into his bassinet, and then they headed back to Karen's room so she could see him.

Ray walked the baby back in, and he told Karen he'd be back because he wanted to go and call Leila. She just nodded because the nurse was handing her the baby. Ray went outside of the hospital and called Leila, and she quickly answered.

"Rayshon," she answered. "I'm a nervous wreck. What's happening? Did she have the baby?"

"He's here, and he's a big boy—eight pounds and four ounces, and he's twenty-one inches long."

"Wow, he's huge. Way bigger than RJ and Rave. I'm dying to know, does he look like you or the kids?" she asked nervously.

"I can't tell right now, Lei—he looks so much like Karen."

"Oh God," she cried. "You have to do the test right away."

"I know because he is so beautiful and innocent, and I don't want to get attached to him and then find out he's not mine."

"Did you guys pick a name?"

"Well, of course, you know what she wanted, but I explained to her crazy ass that it would be stupid to do that, so I think she's going with Shon. I don't know, though. We haven't named him yet."

"Are you going to give him Johnson?" Leila asked.

"I guess. What do you think I should do?"

"Well, if he's yours, he's a Johnson, so the right thing to do is to give it to him, and if later, you find out otherwise, you can have it changed, right?"

"Yeah, I guess," he said, looking down and rubbing his head.

"Can you send me a picture of him," she said, and he said he would. When he got back upstairs, he took a few pictures and sent them to Leila's phone.

She replied, It can't be. At least I hope not. I don't C any resemblance to you or the kids.

He was only a couple of hours old, so it was just too soon to tell.

When Ray left the hospital, he called Leila and begged her to let him come over, and after some pleading, she gave in and let him come home. When he walked in, she was on the sofa, sleeping.

"Baby," he whispered.

"Hey," she said when she opened her eyes.

"Hey, honey, hey," he said, and they hugged. She sobbed, and he knew why, so he just held his wife. "I know, baby, I know," he said, and let her cry.

Chapter Thirty-four

It had been six weeks, and the baby was growing so fast, and they still hadn't done the test. They had two appointments, but somehow, Karen couldn't make it, and she refused to let Ray take him without her. The first time she wasn't feeling well, and the second time, she said it had slipped her mind. Leila had seen the baby and even held him, and she kept telling Rayshon that that baby wasn't his, but he knew that she wanted it not to be so bad that she may have subconsciously not seen any resemblance.

Ray was at work in his office, and he came across the letter again. He opened it and called Dr. Vernon because he didn't know how to read his results. The nurse told him that the doctor was with a patient, and she'd have him call him back. Ray was about to get back out on the floor when Karen walked in with the baby in his carrier.

"Karen, what a surprise," he said, taking the baby's carrier out of her hand and putting it on his desk. The baby was awake and smiling, and as beautiful as he was, he was missing something—Ray's features. He even looked at RJ's and Rayven's baby pictures, and he wondered why the baby didn't look like them either. He settled with the fact that he just took after Karen and let it go and started to bond with him.

"Well, we just left the hospital. They got Shon's sample, and here is your paperwork to go in and give them yours," she said, handing him an envelope.

"Why didn't you call me? I would have met you over there."

"Well, I had to go by there for a visit for myself, so I took the initiative to get the ball rolling. In a few weeks, we'll have the results, and then we can get past all your doubts, and your wife can stop saying my baby looks nothing like her kids," Karen said with attitude. She and Leila were stressing Ray out. He just wanted the results so that they could move on to wherever they were going to be as a family.

"Okay, cool. I'll run by there as soon as I get a break."

"Okay, just go to the lab with this paperwork, and they will do what needs to be done," she smiled.

"All right, no problem," he said and picked up the baby. "Hey, there, li'l man. Your dad is not at all the jerk your mom says I am, so don't listen to her," he joked, and the baby smiled.

"I don't call you a jerk—maybe I've said asshole," she said.

"Hey, don't be cussing around my kid," he said, and she smiled.

"Yeah, he is your kid," she said, and Ray put him back in his seat.

"I gotta go. I know Lauren is here waiting," he said, talking about a client. He grabbed the baby car seat to walk them to the door. He said he'd stop by later before going home to see the baby, and then she left.

Ray finished up his morning and ran across to the hospital to do his lab work. He was so happy to finally be taking care of this and getting it out of the way. As he approached, he saw Katrina, and he wondered what she was doing there.

"Kat," he said.

"Ray, how are you?" she said, and they did a quick hug.

"I'm fine, what are you doing here?"

"Well, my boyfriend works here, and I'm waiting for him so that we can go to lunch. What are you doing here?"

"Well, I'm sure Cherae knows and told you that I had a little hiccup in my marriage, and as a result, I have a six-week-old little boy that I'm getting tested to make sure he's mine."

"To be honest, yes, I heard but didn't know all the details. Heard the baby momma is crazier than I was," she said, and they laughed.

"Yeah, she's a little nuts, but my son is here now."

"Well, if he's your son, you take it cheerfully. If he's not, crack open a bottle," she joked.

"Either way, I know I won't be celebrating. Relieved but not celebrating. The damage is already done," he said sadly.

"At least Leila is one of the good ones. She has stayed with your ass through the good, the bad, and the ugly," she said, and Ray smiled.

"Yea, she's a good one, but this time, she didn't," Ray said, and put his head down in shame.

"Damn, I'm sorry to hear that. I thought since you're still wearing your ring, that things were okay."

"No, I'm wearing it because I'm still married, and I'm praying that we work this thing out," he said, and a guy approached the two of them.

"Wait, this is my boyfriend. Ray, this is Cordell, and Cordell, this is Rayshon."

"Hey, Rayshon, heard a lot, I mean, a lot about you," he said, and Ray was surprised.

"Really?"

"Yeah, they say letting go of the past helps for a better future, so Cordell was a part of my healing. Therefore, he knows everything about you," she said, and Cordell grabbed her hand.

"And you still stayed," Rayshon joked with him.

"Yep, it was hard work, but she's worth it," he said, and Katrina smiled.

"Well, Cordell and I are going to head down to the cafeteria and have our usual. It was really good to see you, Ray, and good luck with everything. I hope things work out for the best," she smiled.

"Thanks, Kat. You take care, and, Cordell, nice meeting you, man," he said. Then Ray proceeded to handle his business. He was nervous, but he knew that the test had to be done.

Chapter Thirty-five

Ray sat at his desk, going over and over the events of the night he and Karen made Shon. He kept asking himself why he didn't remember the entire episode. He thought about it more and more and just couldn't comprehend why everything about that night was so chopped up. He knew he had a couple of Long Islands, but never had he ever felt that feeling, and he wondered if Karen added a little something "extra" to his drink. "Naw, it can't be," he said and tried to shake it off, but he remembered that night being like no other night, and he knew he had been drunk on several occasions, but not so drunk to not remember events that took place, so he called Leila with his theory. Hell, Karen was a nurse, so it was possible, he thought. When he called, Leila wasn't trying to hear that, so he went by the house to have a face to face with her.

"You're telling me that she drugged you?"

"Yes, she is a fucking nurse, baby. She works at the hospital, so she can get her hands on any drug she wants," he said. And the look on Leila's face was incredulous.

"Rayshon, really? You expect me to believe that bullshit? Do you take me for a fool?"

"Leila, I'm serious. I know you're mad and hate me right now, but, baby, believe me. I would have never slept with the woman in my right mind. I know you think that

I was fucking her, but, Leila, I promise you I wasn't," he said sincerely. He knew it was going to take a miracle for her to believe him. "All I know is that I have drunk a gallon of liquor and been totally fucked up, but I've never been so bad that I can't remember bustin' a nut," he said and caught himself because he was talking to his wife. He thought his theory was crazy, but he wanted her to consider it.

"Okay, Rayshon, I hate to admit it, but I believe you. I believe that you were not fucking her on a regular, okay, but you fucked her once to make this little boy," Leila said, looking down at the tiles on the floor.

"That may not be true, Leila. If she drugged me, there's a chance that nothing happened, Leila, and Shon could be someone else's kid. You know what? I'm going to take Shon to a different doctor and have the test done again."

"You think that's necessary, Rayshon? I mean, she can't make him your son if he's not."

"Nope, but she works at that damn hospital, and if she can get a hold of some substance to drug me, I know she may have a way to get in that system. What if she alters the results?" he said, and Leila knew he was right.

"Damn, Ray, you are so right," Leila nodded, and then took another sip of her Merlot.

"I know, baby," he said, walking up behind her and wrapping his arms around her, and she didn't fight him. "Baby, I am so sorry for this big old mess that I got us in," he said and kissed her neck.

"I know, Ray, but this doesn't mean that we are back together, okay? Let's just get our own test done, and, hopefully, we can leave this big-ass, hot mess behind," she said, and he held her tighter.

"I miss you so much, Leila. Can I please come home, and we work this out together?" he asked, and he almost died when he heard her reply.

"Yes, we can do this together, okay? You can come home, Rayshon," she said.

"Oh my God, thank you, baby, thank you," he said, kissing the back of her head. He turned her to face him and kissed her passionately.

"Have you been with her, Rayshon, since you and I have been separated? Have you touched her or been with her?" she asked, and he thought that was a ridiculous question. He had spent every moment of his day trying to come back home.

"No, no, no, baby. I love you more than anything in this world. I love my kids, and I've never wanted her, Leila. I want you and my family. I never wanted to be with Karen, Leila—never. That night should have never happened," he explained with tears in his eyes. He held her and was grateful that she was letting him come back.

"Okay," she said and then polished off her glass of wine. She went up and kissed her kids good night, but when she got into the shower, she sobbed and prayed that Ray was telling her the truth.

She climbed in bed with him and had a strong urge to make love to him. Her mind and body had to be assured that he was still hers, and he wasn't going anywhere. After they made love, she lay in his arms and asked the question that she was sure he didn't want to answer.

"Why couldn't you tell me in the beginning, Ray? I mean, maybe things would have gone down differently," she said, and he squeezed her tighter.

"I was so afraid of losing you, Leila. We had just gotten back together, and you came out of your mouth talking about divorcing me, and I was so scared if I'd answered you that you'd leave."

"I understand your reason, but if I wanted to leave you, Rayshon, it wouldn't have mattered if you told me then or later. I just feel like a fool. Like I was played by my husband and his pregnant mistress," she cried.

"Shhh, Leila, please, baby. I was wrong for not telling you, but I don't take you for a fool. I just prolonged the pain, and trust, I wish I could have spared you this pain," he said, holding her. "Please, Leila, I know I'm asking a lot, but please don't leave me. If this baby is mine, it's going to change everything, and I don't want you to hate me."

"I'm not leaving, Rayshon, and no matter what you did, I could never hate you," she said and closed her eyes. She asked God again to help her as they lay there in silence.

"Thank you, Leila," he said and kissed her on the side of her head. She fell asleep, and he lay there staring at a picture on Leila's nightstand of her holding li'l Ray in her arms when he was just a tiny baby. He thought about how happy he was to become a dad and to have a son, and now, he had another son, and he hated himself for not feeling the same way he felt about RJ. He blinked back the tears and asked God one more time to make this nightmare disappear. He prayed that the results proved the baby *not* to be his son.

The next day, Ray went inside to get the baby while Leila waited in the car. They drove to Dr. Bryce's office, and while they sat in the waiting room, they both kept trying to find a trace of Ray in Shon, but neither one of them saw it. He had Ray's complexion now, but at birth, he was high yellow like Karen. Now, his complexion was darker, maybe Rayven's tone, but that was it.

The nurse called them back and did a swab, and then they went in to talk to Dr. Bryce, who told them that he would try to have the results in as quickly as possible. They rode home, holding hands and confident that they did the right thing. It was just a matter of time before they got the truth.

Chapter Thirty-six

Ray and Leila met Karen at South Suburban Hospital. Karen walked in with a huge grin on her face, and Leila just looked at her with disgust. She handed Ray the baby and signed their names on the list. Then they went to have a seat to wait for their names to be called.

"You seem pretty happy today," Leila said, looking at Karen.

"Well, I have a reason to be happy," she said and looked at Leila with an evil grin.

"I wouldn't be smiling so hard if I were you," Leila said, and Rayshon tapped her leg.

"Come on, babe, let's not do this," he said, encouraging her not to exchange words with Karen.

"No, Ray, it's cool. We're finally going to get the test results, so she can stop denying my kid just because he doesn't look like her damn kids."

"Oh, did you forget? He doesn't look a damn thing like my husband, either," Leila spat, and before Karen could reply, their name was called.

"Well, we'll see in a moment, won't we?" Karen said and rolled her eyes. Rayshon asked Leila to wait and let him and Karen go back and get the test results read. She agreed. When they went back into the office, the lab tech asked them to take a seat, and then he opened a file.

"Well?" Ray said, eager to hear the results.

"Congratulations, Mr. Johnson. Shon is definitely your son," he said, and Karen jumped out of the chair.

"I told you, I told you, I told you," she yelled, and Rayshon kissed the baby with tears in his eyes.

He looked at the lab tech and had to ask, "Are you sure? Is there any way that the results could be wrong or altered?" he asked.

"Are you fucking kidding me right now, Rayshon?" Karen snapped, aggravated.

"Look, Karen, I have to know," he said, looking at her, and she sat down.

"Give it a rest, Rayshon," she huffed.

"Mr. Johnson, we always run our test twice, and the results came back a little over 99 percent, both times."

"So, he's my son?" he asked again.

"Yes, and here is your copy," he said, handing him an envelope. "And here is yours," he said, giving it to Karen.

"Can we have a second, Doc?" Ray asked.

"Sure. Take all the time you need," he said and left them alone.

"Finally," she said, smiling and standing to leave, but Ray stopped her.

"Karen, I hope that you didn't alter these results."

"Ray, seriously? Come on, I don't have access to do such a thing, and if I did, the hospital would know that I logged into the system. No way could I get away with that, Rayshon. Why are you still acting so suspicious? He's your son, and now that we have the truth, you need to tell that wife of yours to show me some respect," she demanded.

He opened the envelope and read the results as he prayed that he'd get the other test results soon and that they would state otherwise.

Karen walked out into the waiting room, and Leila stood as soon as she saw her.

"Allow me to give you the good news. Shon is your husband's son, and from this day forward, you will treat me with respect, and if you dare try to stop Ray from seeing his child, you *will* have to deal with me," Karen said, and Leila got in her face.

"You know what, Karen? Enjoy this day because you do *not* fool me. You have wanted my man from day one, and your schemes and lies and deception to get him didn't work. I don't know how you managed to pull this little charade off, but we'll see who has the last laugh," she hissed.

"Looks to me like I will," Karen replied. Rayshon walked up, and Leila looked him in the eyes.

"Is it true?" she asked him.

"Yes, according to this," he said, holding up the envelope. Shon is 99.7 percent a match," he said, and Leila's eyes glossed over from the tears.

Regardless of whether you like it, Leila, I'm going to be a part of Ray's life for a *very* long time," Karen spat.

"Correction. My son will, *not* you," Ray said and moved close to Leila and put his arm around her.

"Yes, let's just clear this up now. You will *never* have my man, Karen, and understand this . . . Every time you see *his* face, you will see *my* face," Leila spat and walked away. "Rayshon, handle this, and I'll be in the car," she said and kept walking.

"God, she gets on my damn nerves," Karen said, and Ray just looked at her.

"Karen, I know you put something in my drink, and I know you planned this pregnancy, and for that, I will never trust a thing that comes out of your mouth."

"I don't know what you're talking about," Karen said, holding her baby close to her face, and Ray looked at him and thought the same thing Leila thought. What if she didn't alter the test? Shon could be his, so he just changed the subject.

"Whatever, Karen, we'll talk later about . . . custody, visitation, and child support," he said, leaning in to kiss the baby. "Bye, little guy, your dad has to go," he said, and Karen couldn't help but smile.

"Ray, things can be good, you know," she said, looking in his eyes.

"They will be. I may have been a lousy husband, but I'm a damn good dad. Just keep in mind that this relationship between you and me is all about Shon, so don't even attempt any tricks or games, Karen, I mean it. I am not going to have craziness in my house or my life, understood?" he said, and she nodded. "I'll talk to you later," he said and walked away.

Karen was bursting with joy. She couldn't wait to tell her girl Leslie her wonderful news, so she reached in her pocket and took out her phone. Leslie told her to meet her in the cafeteria because she was on lunch break. Karen sat at the table, waiting for her, and smiled at the cute couple at the table that sat a few feet from where she sat. "Leslie, it's done. I did it, girl. I did it," she said with excitement as soon as Leslie sat down.

"What, girl, what?" Leslie asked.

"Girl, Rayshon is going to be mine for sure now," she said, grinning and bursting with excitement.

"How so? I thought you said he and Leila got back together."

"They did, but we just got the test results, and I told you my plan was foolproof," she said so happily. "You should have seen the look on Leila's face. That bitch was too through. I'm going to make her life a living hell," Karen said proudly.

"Oh my God, Karen, tell me how in the hell did you switch the results? I'm like—" she said, then paused. "How in the hell did you do it?" Leslie quizzed.

"Girl, I told you that I had it all under control," she said, and the look on Leslie's face said she wanted the juicy details.

"Okay, I see, but tell me," she said, and Karen tried to talk low.

"Well, you remember when his son broke his arm?" she asked, and Leslie nodded. "I swabbed him and kept the swab. I gave it to the lab, and now he can never deny my son again. The results came back 99.7 percent, girl," she boasted.

"I'm going to get him for sure now. I know Leila felt stupid when we told her, and I wanted to laugh in her damn face," she said, and Leslie looked at her like she was insane.

"Karen, I can't believe you. I mean, you can't continue to lie like this. I mean, damn . . ." she said.

"Leslie, what? You knew what I was planning to do. You know how much I love Rayshon. I had to do something," she beamed. Karen was so proud of what she had accomplished.

"I know, I just didn't think you'd take it this far."

"Les, really? You think I drugged him, inseminated myself, and walked around with this baby in my womb, ruining my figure not to go all the way? My mission is to get Rayshon, and nothing has changed," she said.

"Karen, you sound like a damn crazy person right now, and I can't do this anymore, okay? How many times are you going to go down this road? As soon as one man shows you an ounce of respect or attention, you transform into this psycho stalker chick. And, no, I didn't think you'd take it this far, and I can't be your best friend on the sidelines, cheering for you to destroy people's lives anymore. I suggest you tell the truth, and for Shon's sake, get some help, Karen. It's been married man after married man since junior high," she said, and Karen wanted to slap her face.

"Are you crazy, Leslie? I can't do that, and I don't need help. You and my mother—I swear. I finally got him where I want him, and it's only a matter of time before I make him mine, and that's final for me. I have never wanted any of those motherfuckers this bad, Les," she said, and Leslie was dead serious when she said she was done with her crazy-ass behavior.

"Karen, if you don't tell him, I will. I'll tell him everything. I will even inform him that you can't even get an erection on Versed, so he can know that he didn't even have sex with you," she said and stood to leave.

"Tell him, and you will no longer work in this hospital, Leslie. You can kiss your RN license goodbye," she said and stood. "I see you have forgotten that *you* are the one who took the Versed for me, and that's not the only time you've swiped drugs, so my advice to you is to keep your mouth shut, or I will let them know about your little 'addiction,'" she threatened.

Afraid, Leslie just looked at her. "You wouldn't," she cried with a look of pure panic on her face.

"Oh, but I would," she returned, and then she grabbed the baby and left. She felt like a huge weight had been lifted off her shoulders, and all she had to do now was figure out a way to get her man *and* keep Leslie quiet.

Chapter Thirty-seven

Katrina called Cher, but she couldn't reach her. She left her five messages telling her it was urgent and to call her back right away. Then she went by the gym looking for Ray, but he wasn't there, so she rushed over to Cher's office, and they said she was out showing some property. Katrina was walking around wondering what to do and decided she'd go back to work and just wait for Cher to return her call.

After her shift, she called Cher, and she finally answered.

"Hey, Kat, what's the big emergency, girl?"

"I need to get a hold of Rayshon," she said.

"Kat, come on. I thought you were over that, and you know I can't give you his number."

"I am, Cher, but this is about Karen, the one that claims he's her baby's daddy," she said.

"Who and what? What's going on, sis?"

"Cher, please, I can't explain right now. I just need to call him right away or even Leila," she said with desperation in her voice.

"Look, you know I can't give you their numbers, but what I will do is give Leila a call, and then I'll ask her to call you," she said, and Katrina agreed with that.

"Just hurry," she said and hung up. Cher dialed Leila and left her a voicemail telling her to call her back. She scrolled through her phone and realized she didn't have Rayshon's number, so she hoped Leila would call her soon.

   Leila was lying in her bed, resting. She had an exhausting day, and she didn't want to talk to anyone. She was terrified that the results were accurate, and what they thought was a lie wasn't. She wasn't sure if she could live with it. She was also angry as hell and starting to feel anger toward Rayshon.

   "Lei," he whispered.

   "Yes?" she said softly.

   "You gotta eat something, honey," he said, but she wasn't hungry or in the mood to talk to him.

   "I'm not hungry, Rayshon," she said.

   "Leila, I know you are mad and hurt, but there is still a chance that she's lying," he tried to say, and Leila sat up.

   "What if she's not? I wanted to believe all these horrible things about that woman, Rayshon, and how she was crazy and did all this damage to my marriage, but the fact of the matter is, it was you," she blasted.

   "Whoa, Leila, baby. You know I never wanted any of this to happen, and you know I hate putting you and our family through this entire ordeal," he said, and she believed him, but that didn't ease her pain.

   "I know, Ray, and I'm not sure if I can really handle this. I mean, I thought I could, but the result hit me hard. I was so busy telling myself that she was a liar and that the baby wasn't yours and how the test was going to get her out of our lives, but after what happened earlier, I'm scared to death, Rayshon, and I don't know if I can do this," she cried. He reached for her, but she pulled back.

"Leila, please," he said and tried to hold her again, but she stood.

"I know you're sorry, Rayshon, and I forgive you for everything, but I just don't know right now. I have too many mixed emotions about this," she said and walked toward the door.

"Where are you going?"

"By Jay's. I need some air," she said, and she left. Ray threw the remote across the room. It crashed against the wall. He knew from the silent ride home that Leila was upset. He knew that those first set of results could be genuine, so both of them were terrified.

When Leila got to Jay's, she was surprised to see Devon sitting at the bar alone. They hadn't seen much of each other lately, and he rarely got out of the car when he picked up and dropped off Deja because they wanted to keep Christa and Rayshon from freaking out.

"Is this seat taken?" Leila asked, and Devon looked up.

"Leila! What a pleasant surprise. Have a seat," he said, and she climbed onto the stool as Tony came over to get her drink order.

"So, what brings you out tonight, and where's your wife?"

"Needed some air, and Christa wanted to pack alone."

"Pack? What are you talking about?" she asked, and Tony set her drink in front of her.

"It didn't work, Lei," he said and put his head down.

"Aw, Devon, I'm so sorry," she said.

"It's okay. You know, it was bound to end. As long as you exist, Christa would have been insecure. No matter how good I tried to be to her, we'd always end up arguing about you. She wanted to rid the house of everything because she knew that everything reminded me of you.

Do you know she threw out all of our pots and pans because one day I said that you said that a certain pan was perfect for steaming fish?"

"The red one, right?"

"Yep, the red one and that set her off, and the next day when I came home, she had all new cookware. When I told her that was insane, she blew up and said she was tired of you being in our marriage, so I told her that she was the one that was always bringing you up or comparing herself to you. I mean, everything would be, *'Does Leila clean like this?'* or *'Does Leila do it like that? I betcha Leila would have done it differently,'*" he said, speaking in his Christa's voice.

"I mean, it was so redundant, and I just got tired of her throwing your name in my face. Tired of her constantly comparing you two and tired of her asking me if I was sure that I was over you," he said and took a sip of his drink.

"Wow, I'm sorry, Devon, and trust, I know what you were going through," she said, feeling bad for him.

"Well, I'll be all right, I guess. At first, I will admit I started dating her to make you jealous. Back then, it was all about you, but Christa is a great woman, and in a short time, I did grow to love her. I wish I could have proven my love for her or been better to her. I don't know, I didn't want to lose her," he said, and they sat in silence for a moment. "Why are you here? Where's Mr. Johnson?"

"Home, as you and the world know by now, I got baby momma drama," she said, and he nodded.

"Yeah, I heard."

"We got the test results today, and I was just expecting them to be negative," she said, and her eyes teared up.

"Wow, I'm sorry, sweetheart," he said, rubbing her back.

"It's okay. I just don't know if I'm strong enough to accept it."

"You are, Leila. It's not the end of the world."

"I know, but it hurt so damn bad," she said, and he gave her a napkin from the stack on the bar to wipe her eyes.

"It'll get easier," he said.

"I hope so, because Karen is a thorn in my side, for real." Suddenly, Karen walked in with another young lady in tow. "Speak of the damn devil," she murmured, and Karen looked right at her. She walked in her direction, and Leila wondered why she was coming over.

"Hey, Leila, how are you?"

"Fine, Karen," she spat.

"And you are?" she asked Devon.

"Devon," he said, shaking her extended hand.

"So, you're the infamous Devon. I heard so much about you. Not a surprise to see you here with Leila since y'all are so close and all."

"Shouldn't you be home with your child?"

"Shouldn't you be home with your husband?" Karen retorted. "Oh, I meant with my baby's daddy," she said, and Leila wanted to punch her in the throat.

"Devon, I'm leaving," Leila said, getting up, and Devon got up too. She moved quickly to the door, and Karen waved bye with an evil smirk.

Chapter Thirty-eight

When Leila finally made it home, Rayshon was sleeping on the sofa with Rayven on his chest. Leila gently picked her up and took her to her crib, and then returned to wake Rayshon. When she shook him, he grabbed her arm and pulled her down on top of him and held her tightly. He got the text from Karen earlier, saying that she saw Leila and Devon hugged up at Jay's, and he deleted it because he didn't believe her. He knew she was trying to stir up some mess, so he laughed at the foolish attempt to get him angry with Leila.

They lay on the sofa for the rest of the night, and the next morning, Leila's phone woke her up. She looked at the ID, saw it was Cher. She put it down without answering and lay back on Ray's chest. She dozed off again, and then her phone rang once more, so she went ahead, got up, and took the call.

"Good morning," Cher sang.

"Hey, Cher, what's up?" Leila said groggily.

"I'm sorry to wake you, Leila. I thought you'd be up with the kids."

"It's okay. I gotta get them up soon," she said, going for the orange juice. "What do I owe this early-morning honor?"

"Well, Kat called me yesterday and said she had something to tell Rayshon about Karen. She wanted one of you guys to give her a call," Cher said, and Leila went for a pen.

"What's going on?"

"I'm not sure, but it sounded important."

"What's the number?" she asked, and Cher gave it to her. She repeated it back and told Cher she'd give Ray the message. Leila ran up and got the kids up, so they could get dressed for school. When she came down, she started breakfast, and Ray walked into the kitchen.

"Good morning, babe," he said and leaned in and kissed her cheek.

"Good morning," she said, moving around the kitchen. He leaned against the counter and rubbed his head. She looked up at him and saw the stressed look on his face beneath his neatly trimmed beard and mustache. She hated what he was going through, but he was partly to blame. She put the carton of eggs on the counter and walked over to him, and this time, she hugged him.

He grabbed her, leaned in, and cried on her shoulder. His tears wet her hair and the side of her neck, and she wrapped her arms around him. "I'm so sorry, baby," he cried, and she knew he was.

"It's okay, Ray. We're going to be fine," she said because she could see the pain behind his eyes, and she knew her husband was, overall, a great man.

"I wish I could take it back," he cried.

"I know, Ray, baby, I know," she said as li'l Ray walked in.

"Daddy, are you crying?" he asked with his head tilted and a look of confusion on his little face.

"Yeah, li'l man," he said, wiping his eyes. "Daddy's just a little upset about something."

"Like what? What can I do to make you feel better?" he asked, and Ray picked him up.

"Nothing, baby. Daddy's going to be okay. Run upstairs and make sure your sister is getting ready, okay?" he said, and RJ took off as soon as he put him down.

"We're going to have to tell them," she said.

"I know, Leila, but I wanna wait till after we hear from Dr. Bryce's office," he insisted, and then he started to help her get the kids breakfast.

"I honestly think the results are going to be the same," she said softly.

"Leila, don't say that. That is my only hope, and I don't feel it in my heart. I just have to be absolutely sure before I tell my children about the baby," he said. Then Deja walked in on their conversation.

"What baby?" she asked.

"None of your little business, that's what, baby," Leila said to her because Deja was a nosy smarty-pants. "Make sure your brother is dressed. Breakfast will be ready soon," she said, and Deja knew that meant get out of the kitchen. "I'm going to go up and get Rave. Can you take it from here?" Leila asked.

"Yeah, I got it."

"Oh, Cherae called this morning. Said Katrina needs to talk to you about Karen."

"About what?"

"I'm not sure, but she said Katrina said it was important. I can't imagine what that's about. Considering Katrina is your ex-stalker, I assume she's not crazy enough to try any shit again."

"Katrina isn't on that anymore."

"I know. Just call her and see what it's about," Leila said and went on upstairs, and then Ray finished cooking breakfast for the kids. He got them fed and put them on the school bus. He came back and showered and dressed for work, and when he kissed Leila goodbye, he made her promise him that she was not going to leave him over this, and she reminded him that divorce wasn't an option.

Chapter Thirty-nine

When Ray walked into his office, he realized he forgot Katrina's number, so he called Leila for it, but she didn't pick up. He was about to get started when Karen walked in with the baby, and Ray wondered why she was there.

"Karen," he asked, looking at her strangely, "what are you doing here?"

"My mom can't watch the baby, and I have no one else to watch him on this short notice."

"And you bring him here? Karen, I have a client in five minutes," he said.

"But you have a daycare here," she protested and pushed the baby in his direction.

"Which doesn't open for another hour," he said, looking at her like she was crazy.

"Rayshon, I just got back to work. I have no more time available to take off, and you need to keep your son," she said, and he looked at his watch. His temples flared, and he knew he had to ask his wife to watch his son.

"Look, I'll take him, and he can hang at the desk with Catrice. Leila is going to have to keep him."

"Oh, hell no," she disputed.

"Karen, listen, Leila stays home with my daughter, and she is the only one that can come now and pick him up, so if you don't want my wife to watch him, you need to figure something else out," he said.

She looked at her watch. "Ray, if my child has so much as a scratch on him—" she tried to say, but he cut her off.

"Karen, don't even go there. You know damn well she wouldn't do anything to hurt him. He's my child, crazy ass, and my wife wouldn't harm him," he said, and she handed the baby and his bag over to Ray.

"Okay, my shift ends at five," she said and hurried out. Ray was about to call Leila again, but he had to run out to ask his client to give him a minute. He set the baby seat on the floor behind the counter and asked Catrice to call his house for him, and then he got his client started on the treadmill. When he came back to the desk, Catrice said she didn't answer. She assured Ray she'd keep an eye on Shon and keep trying Leila, so he went back to his client.

Twenty minutes later, Ray got a page that Leila was on the line, and when he told her about Karen dropping Shon off on him, Leila was pissed. She dressed and dressed Rayven and went over to pick up Shon. When she got home, she told herself that she could do it . . . She could care for her husband's baby. She made up her mind that she wasn't going to let this destroy her family.

When Tabitha got there, Leila thought it would be best to get the baby out of the house before the kids got off the bus. She went back to the gym, and she and the babies were in the office when Ray came in. He was happy to see them.

"Wow, baby, how was he?" he asked, picking him up first, and Leila got a little jealous because Rayven was in her chair too.

"He was fine, and why did you pick him up first?" she asked, and Rayshon laughed.

"Seriously, Leila, it wasn't on purpose. It's just that you're used to having Rave, but this was your first day with Shon," he said, putting him down and then picking up his little princess.

"I hope my last," she said.

He nodded in agreement with her. "Yeah, that was crazy what Karen pulled this morning. I'm going to suggest she find a daycare if her momma's going to pull moves like this," he told her, putting Rayven down.

"Yea, then she's going to want more money," she said.

"Maybe, but he has to go somewhere that's reliable."

"True because I can't do this every day," she expressed.

"I know, baby, and thank you for watching him today. I can imagine that it wasn't easy," he said and sat at his desk.

"No problem." She stood to leave. "I'm going to head home. Will you be on time for dinner?" she asked.

"Yeah, I should be. Karen will be picking Shon up about 5:30, I guess. I'm going to take him into the daycare till she gets here," he said, and she leaned in and kissed him.

"Okay, later, babe," Leila said and grabbed Rayven and left. Ray took Shon and signed him into the facility daycare. Karen picked him up, and Ray told her to look for a daycare, and as Leila said, she asked if he would pay, and, of course, he said yes. He told her that he wouldn't be by after work since he got a chance to see Shon already, and just as he was ready to leave and head home for dinner, Katrina walked in.

Chapter Forty

"Hey, Ray," she said nervously.

"Kat, what's going on?" he asked, surprised to see her.

"I know this is weird, but can we talk?" she said in a serious manner.

"Yeah, sure, what's up?" he asked.

"It's kinda private. Can we talk in your office?"

He wanted to say no, but he got the sense that she was not there to ask him about hooking up, so he told her to follow him. They went into his office, and he hesitated, but he closed the door anyway.

"Have a seat," he said, and she sat down. "So, what's up?" he asked when he took a seat at his desk, and she cleared her throat.

"Ummm, Ray, I know this may not be my place, but yesterday, I overheard something that I think you should know," she began, and he leaned forward on his desk.

"What? What is it? You sound so serious."

"Well, I went by the hospital yesterday to meet Cordell for lunch, and when I was sitting in the cafeteria waiting, I saw Karen. I mean, I think I saw Karen."

"You know Karen?"

"No, I don't know her, but a woman was sitting next to me with a baby boy, and she met with a friend and talked about how happy she was for pulling off her 'plan.'"

"Pulling what off? I don't follow."

"She said how she got the test results back and how she was going to make Rayshon her man and make Leila's life a living hell, and I only know one Rayshon and one Leila," she said, and he was still lost. He knew Karen wanted him and thought she was going to get him eventually, and he also knew she hated Leila.

"Okay," he said and waited for her to give him more information.

"Well, I also heard her say that you were a match because she swabbed your son when he broke his arm, and that's the swab she gave the lab, and that's why it came back a match," she said . . . and Ray's mouth dropped.

"You're kidding me, right?" he said, blinking a hundred times a second.

"I wish I were. She was talking to someone named Leslie, and she mentioned the Versed, and Karen told her she would tell the hospital that Leslie took the Versed for her. It turns out she has some dirt on her friend taking pills from the hospital for her addiction, and she threatened to expose her. The fear in Leslie's eyes was serious," she said. Rayshon was speechless.

"I'll be damned. This bitch not only drugged me, but she swabbed RJ months before the pregnancy, Katrina. How is that possible?" Ray asked, confused.

"I knew you'd ask that question, so I asked Cordell, and he explained that DNA could live for years, and she probably stored the swab in a safe place, and that's how she used it," Katrina explained. Ray wanted to shout. He was relieved but angry as hell.

"Do you know what kinda hell Karen has put my wife and me through? Thank God I never introduced that little boy to my kids. They'd be crazy confused. God, I'm so happy. Leila and I did a test on our own," he informed her.

"So, you did do another test? That's great because I asked Cordell if he'd run another one for you, and he would have done it for you, Ray, because I overheard something more," she said.

"What?" he asked, and Katrina was hesitant in her response.

"Well, according to Leslie, y'all never even had sex. She said that you couldn't even get an erection on Versed, and she told Karen that she would tell you that y'all never had sex. That's when Karen turned into psycho Karen, and Leslie ran off," she said, telling Ray everything. He was in total disbelief. He had been had, and he couldn't believe his ears.

He sat there for a few moments to gather his thoughts because he was so dumbfounded from what he had just heard.

"Thanks, Kat," was all he could say after hearing everything she said.

"So, what are you going to do in the meantime?"

"Play her game and humiliate her in a public place. I want to bring the same shame to her that she brought to my wife and me," he said, and Katrina understood.

"Well, Ray, you don't know how sorry I am, and I hated to have to tell you, but I couldn't keep something like that from you," she said and got up.

"Thanks, Kat. After all we've been through, I would have never thought we'd see a day like this," he said, and she extended her hand, but he hugged her.

"You're welcome, Ray, and I know I told Leila I was sorry, but I never told you. I'm truly sorry for the foul and crazy shit I did to you back then," she said, and he squeezed her a little tighter.

"Apology accepted," he said, and then he let her go. She left, and he couldn't wait to get home and tell Leila.

Chapter Forty-one

Rayshon and Leila left Dr. Bryce's office with the real results in hand. Rayshon was not the father of Karen's baby, and he couldn't believe something so crazy had actually happened to him. He couldn't comprehend how he could attract crazy-ass women. First, he went through it with Katrina, but thank God she was now off the crazy list and now, Karen. For Shon's sake, Rayshon hoped that Karen got some help.

"So, how do you want to do this?" Leila asked.

"Well, I was thinking I'd have a big party in my honor to celebrate how stupid I was for believing her and hurting my family and spring it on her during my, '*I'm so stupid, I let a stalker like Karen make a big-ass fool outta me,*' speech."

"I was thinking something bigger, something grander," she said, and Rayshon wanted to know what she had in mind. When she said what she thought would be a better idea, Ray was shocked.

"Lei, are you serious?"

"Dead serious," she said, and Ray knew that a woman with vengeance on her mind could be deadly.

"I don't know, babe, she may get suspicious," he said, thinking the plan was perfect but thought Karen was too smart to go for it.

"Trust me, baby, she's going to go for it. All she ever wanted was to have you, and trust, she'll do *anything* to have you," she said, and he nodded in agreement. He pulled into their garage, and they went inside to discuss the details of Leila's master plan.

After they ate and did their regular routine, Ray grabbed his coat and keys and headed for the door to get their plan into motion. Leila kissed him and told him to make her believe him, and after he assured her he had it, she let him leave. He knocked on Karen's door. She was surprised, but she let him in.

"Wow, Ray, what brings you by? Your son is already asleep," she said, and he headed for the kitchen as if he lived there. He opened the cabinet and grabbed a glass, then went for the Crown Royal on the counter. She stood watching with a look of confusion on her face.

"Ice," he said, and she went over and grabbed his glass and hit the automatic ice dispenser on the fridge, put a few cubes in, and handed him the glass.

"Ray, what's wrong? What's going on?" she asked again. She stood and watched his every move, trying to play it cool, but Rayshon could see the fear in her eyes, and how she tried to hide her nervousness as he swirled the drink around and took a swallow.

"You were right," he said.

"Right about what?"

"Leila and I don't have a chance because of Shon—and do you know that she had the nerve to tell me to choose between my son and her?" he said. By now, Karen looked confused.

"What happened, Rayshon? I don't follow," she said, and he added more to his drink.

"Can we sit?" he said like he was upset.

"Sure, baby, of course."

"Well, you know the other day when we got Shon's results?" he said.

"Yeah, go on."

"When we got in the car, she started in on me saying that you fixed the results, and she knew you found a way to have the doctor change the results. I told her to give it a rest and that I was tired of her trying to make me deny my son, and that no one altered the test. I told her to accept the truth, and that upset her, of course. I've been on the couch since that night, and tonight, I hung out a little bit after work with Mario, and when I walked in, she accused me of being out with you, fucking around. Even when I denied it, she called me a liar and told me to leave," he said with his head down.

"Oh, Ray, I'm so sorry," she said like she was concerned and genuinely sorry, but he knew damn well that the words that he uttered were music to her ears.

"It's okay, Karen. It's not your fault. I'm just glad that I see her true colors, and after everything, she had the nerve to ask me to choose between her and my son," he said and swallowed more of his drink.

"That was selfish of her, Rayshon. I mean, I can't stand her, but I thought she was better than that," Karen stated. He could see she was trying so hard to hold back her excitement. The nervousness that she had shown had magically disappeared because her dreams were finally coming true.

"Yeah, me too," he said and lay back on the sofa.

"Well, you know you can stay here with us, Ray. You don't have to go. Shon and I would love to have you around," she said, moving closer to him and taking him by the hand.

"I know, Karen, that's sweet of you to offer after how I've treated you," he said, and she cut him off.

"No, Ray, it's okay," she said earnestly.

"I know, Karen, but I think it would be better if I stayed at Mario's for a little while. At least until I can talk to my lawyer," he said.

"Lawyer? Rayshon, what do you mean?"

"She asked me to choose, Karen. I can't be with a woman that would ask me to choose between her and my kid. Come on now, as much as I love Leila, I love my damn kids more," he said, and Karen nodded.

"Hey, I understand, Ray, and I'm sorry. I am happy to know that you love Shon as much as you love your other kids," she expressed.

"Yes, I do, and I'm not going to let a woman come between my kids and me," he said, and she offered him a refill. His mind went back to her spiked drink, so he quickly declined.

"Naw, I'm going to head to Mario's," he said, standing. "Can I look in on my son?" he asked, and she was beaming.

"Sure, go ahead," she said, and he walked down the hall. When he looked in on the baby lying in his crib, Ray did feel a little bit of sadness, because regardless of everything, he did bond with the child, and Shon was an innocent baby, smack dead in the middle of his crazy-ass momma's fantasy world.

He reached in and touched his little head and felt bad because when this was all over, he wouldn't see him anymore. He exited the room and blinked back his tears. Then he headed for the door.

"You leaving?" she asked, approaching him by the door.

"Yeah, I'll see you guys tomorrow," he said and made his exit.

As soon as Ray got into his truck, he called Leila and said, "Plan in motion, baby. She went for it."

Four nights later, Rayshon showed up again with movies and popcorn. She opened the door and jumped up and wrapped her arms around his neck. Karen was so happy because it was finally happening. She had to pinch herself yesterday when Ray showed up to the hospital to take her to lunch.

"Baby, I'm so happy to see you," she said as he walked in.

"Really? I couldn't tell," he joked, and she slapped his arm.

"Come on in, boo. The baby is sleeping. Tonight is just for us," she said, and Rayshon smiled.

"How long has he been asleep? I wanted to see my baby tonight. The last couple of nights, he's been asleep, babe."

"I know, Ray, but he was a little cranky, and I wanted to have a little grown-up time," she said, approaching him seductively.

"Come on, baby, we have plenty of time for that. I just want to relax and watch some movies. My life is stressful enough with Leila in my ear with bullshit. I just want to go in the kitchen and fix me a drink and cuddle on the couch with you," he said, and she smiled and batted her eyes.

"Okay, babe, understood. I'll pop in the movie, and you go fix not only you but me a drink too, and we can chill on the sofa," she said, and he went into the kitchen.

He came back and put their drinks on the table, and he pulled out his phone.

"Baby, I thought tonight was all about us. Why you got the phone?"

"I just had to send a quick text to say good night to my kids so we won't be disturbed." After he put his phone away, they settled on the sofa and didn't talk much as they watched the movie. A little before eleven, he got a phone call from Mario saying that his car wouldn't start, so Ray had to go. Karen was sad, but he assured her that he'd be by the next night, and with that, she walked him to the door.

"So, tomorrow, right?" she asked and wrapped her arms around his neck. He grabbed her ass and gave her a little peck and agreed on seeing her the next day, and she let him leave. She was so happy when she shut the door. She just knew that they were on the road to be a perfect couple.

Chapter Forty-two

"Leila," Rayshon called out when he got in the door.

"Up here," she yelled over the banister, and he raced up the steps. He walked in, and she was getting dressed. He wanted to undress her. It had been two weeks since he had some because he was busy working on making Karen trust that they might have a chance to be together. He wanted this to be over because now, she was coming on to him strong, and he couldn't keep her off him too much longer.

"Wow, it's like you're going on a date, not to confront Leslie," he said because she was looking sexy as hell.

"Yea, well, once I show her the real results and tell her that I know she's the one who stole the Versed and that I will report her if she doesn't help us to bring Karen down, I will bring this sexiness home and do things to you that will make your toes curl."

"Oh, well, you better get going," he said, and she kissed him goodbye. When she arrived, she looked around and spotted Leslie at the bar, so she walked over to her.

"Leslie," she said, and Leslie looked over her shoulder.

"Leila," she said, and Leila sat. She signaled for the bartender and ordered a drink.

"So, did you have trouble finding this place?" she asked, making small talk.

"No, but I'm wondering why you wanted to meet with me," Leslie said and took a sip of her drink.

"Well, it's simple. I would like for you to secretly record your lying friend confessing about drugging my husband, swabbing my son, and trying to destroy my marriage," she said, and Leslie almost spit out her drink.

"What?"

"Oh, you seem shocked. Here's the good part. I know you had something to do with it, and if you don't help me, I'll be happy to tell the hospital that you are the one who stole the Versed that Karen used to drug my husband, and I may also mention that you have a little habit of your own that you are using the hospital to support," she said. The shocked look on Leslie's face said it all.

Leila then took a large envelope from her purse. "Now, you're a nurse, right? And I'm sure you know how to read test results," she said, taking two sheets of paper out. "These are the results from my husband's lab work that showed Versed was in his system the night the so-called baby-making went down, and here are the results from the test our private doctor performed on Shon that says he's *not* Ray's son," she said and handed them to Leslie. As she scanned the documents, her hands began to tremble.

"How . . ." she asked, reading the results. "How did you find all of this out? How do you know it was me that took the Versed?"

"Really, Leslie, you wanna know how? You assisted in doing a horrible thing. You and your crazy-ass friend did a horrible thing to my family—to my husband and me."

"I know, Leila, and I'm so sorry. I knew Karen was out of control, but I couldn't stop her. The day she asked me to get the Versed was the night she had Rayshon over, and the next day, he went back to you. I honestly thought she would just give it a rest and let it go, but she told me she was pregnant a month later. I knew then she was crazy, and I knew the truth would come out, but I had no idea she swabbed your son. I thought for sure she'd be busted after the test. I wanted to tell Rayshon, but she threatened to tell that I took the Versed for her," she explained, but Leila didn't feel sorry for her at all.

"How could you do that, Leslie?"

"I know it was horrible, Leila, and I'm sorry."

"Well, you won't have a problem recording her, will you?"

"I guess I won't," she said, and she put her head down. "So, what did you have in mind?" she asked, and Leila filled her in on all the details. After that, Leslie headed home, and her hands were shaking. Karen was crazy, and she didn't know how she was going to get Karen to rehash the entire story without her being suspicious.

The next evening, Karen and the baby arrived at Leslie's house, and Leslie was nervous as hell. She made sure the camera was in place, and then she opened the door. When Karen walked in, she was smiling and bursting with joy. "Girl, I have good news. I mean, what I'm about to tell you is going to blow your mind, Les," Karen exclaimed.

"Come on in and tell me your good news," Leslie said to a beaming Karen. Leslie already knew the entire story and knew why her psycho friend was glowing.

"Oh, Leslie, I'm the luckiest woman on the planet," she said, pushing her baby's stroller near the sofa, and then she took a seat.

"Really, now?" Leslie said, and joined her on the sofa. She grabbed the bottle of wine that was on the coffee table and filled both glasses.

"Yes, girl, Rayshon came to me last night and said that he wants to marry me and what could be more awesome than that?" she exclaimed, bubbling over. She was all smiles.

"Marriage? Wow. I can see why you're on cloud nine, Karen," she said. She decided not to waste any time getting what she needed on tape. She reached over to her end table and hit the record button on the wireless remote for the recorder and prayed that it started.

"Yes, and nothing—not even Leila's fat ass—can ruin my mood," she said, and they laughed.

Leslie took a sip and then said, "So, swabbing Rayshon's son when he broke his little arm, stealing Versed, drugging him, inseminating yourself with another man's sperm, lying to him about being Shon's dad, and submitting li'l Ray's DNA to get a matching result all paid off, huh?" She smiled, extending her arm to toast, and crazy Karen toasted to that.

"Yep, I guess you can say that. I did what I had to do," she said and clanked Leslie's glass. "I know it was crazy and extreme, but I set out to get my man, and what can I say? Mission accomplished," she said, and Leslie smiled with her crazy ass. Karen had no idea she just got taped admitting that she stole the Versed and not Leslie, and Leslie was feeling relieved. If Karen even attempted to accuse her, she now had proof. All she would say is Karen used her code to take it.

"So, how do you feel?" Leslie asked, now smiling with Karen's demented ass.

"Like I just won the lottery," Karen said, and Leslie knew come Saturday night, that smile would be erased from her crazy face. After Karen left, she called Leila and Rayshon and met them at the gym to give them the recorder. They hooked it up to Rayshon's laptop and took a look. They knew they had all they needed to burst Karen's game wide open.

Chapter Forty-three

Karen opened the door to her king. She was super excited about her night. "Hey, beautiful, you look stunning," Ray said, and Karen smiled.

"Thank you, handsome," she said, and he gave her a soft peck.

"Are you ready?" he asked. "I can't wait to get you to the club and show you the night of your life, beautiful," he smiled.

She blushed. "Am I?" she said and took his hand. She knew Jay's was one of their hangouts, and she couldn't wait to walk in on Rayshon's arm. They got into his truck, and she was beaming the entire ride. She looked and noticed that there was no ring on Ray's finger, and she wanted to dance a jig.

When they arrived, the lot was full, and Karen couldn't wait to get inside. He opened her door and helped her out. She walked to the door with her head held high, and when they got inside, everyone yelled, "Surprise!" and she wondered what the occasion was.

"Oh my God, Ray, what's going on?" she said when she noticed her mom, coworkers, and friends. She thought her mom was watching their son. She smiled because she figured Rayshon had taken care of everything to make her night special.

"It's a party for you. I just wanted to celebrate the mother of my son. After everything I put you through and all the pain I caused you not believing Shon was my son, I just wanted to do something nice for you," he said, and she was outdone.

"Oh, Rayshon, this is so unexpected. Thank you, baby," she said, bursting with joy.

"I know, baby, now enjoy yourself," he said, and they mingled and had a good time. Karen was smiling and having the time of her life . . . until she spotted Leila at the bar sipping on a glass of something, maybe white wine. What in the hell was Leila doing there, she wondered, and her smile faded. She knew if Rayshon saw her, it would probably ruin her night. When she saw Leila approaching, she grabbed Rayshon's arm and smiled.

"Karen, Rayshon," Leila said.

"Leila," Karen returned with a bright smile on her face. "Ray and I are surprised to see you here."

"Well, I heard about your little party through the grapevine, and I wanted to come out and say congratulations on your victory. You saw what you wanted and went for it, and seeing that you're holding on to my man like he's your new bracelet, I'd say your scheme worked," Leila said with a smile and walked away.

"Why did she come?" she asked Rayshon.

"I don't know, babe, but just relax. She won't spoil anything. It's your night," he said, and she looked up and smiled at him. After a few moments, she made her way over to Leila to confront her. She had a feeling she was up to no good, and she wanted to get to the bottom of it.

"Why are you *really* here, Leila?" she barked.

"It's a free country, Karen. I can go where I want. Why are you in my face?"

"I just wanted to tell you to stay out of my man's face. You had your chance, and you threw him out. Now, he's with me," she said, and Leila laughed in her face.

"You are truly pathetic, Karen," Leila continued to giggle and walked away.

Leila went to find Kennedy to see if everything was in place, and Kennedy told her yes. Then Leila walked over to the stage, and when she stood in front of the mic, Johnson, a longtime DJ for Julian and Kennedy, killed the music. When Karen saw her on stage, Leila could see the scowl on her face, but she continued with their plans.

"Good evening, ladies and gentlemen," she said, and everyone turned their attention to the stage. Karen stood still, and her fists were balled up at her side. Leila could see she was furious. "My name is Leila, and I am the woman of the hour man's wife," she said, and people began to whisper.

"Yes, you heard me correctly. Rayshon is my husband," she said, pointing in his direction, and all eyes turned to him and Karen because she was standing at his side. "That handsome guy right over there, standing next to Karen, his baby momma," she said, and everyone continued to whisper, but she continued. "Now, I'm sure most of you know the story. I know there were plenty of rumors and gossip that went around about us and how she took my man and blah blah blah, but I'm here tonight to set the record straight and let everybody in on a little secret," she said. Immediately, Cher came up to the bottom of the stage and handed her a few sheets of paper which Leila held up.

"What I am holding in my left hand here is a copy of the DNA test that was given to my husband and me at South Suburban that states that Karen's son is a match, and he is my husband's son. In my right hand, I am holding a copy of the DNA test results that my husband and I got from our private doctor that states that Karen's son is not a match," she said, and everyone gasped. Karen's vanilla face went pale, and Leila thought she'd pass out, but she kept going.

Infuriated, Karen yelled, "You lying bitch! Rayshon, she's lying. Don't believe her, baby," she pleaded, and he just nodded at Leila to proceed.

"Well, I knew Karen would deny it, so if you all would just take a look at the closest monitor to you, you'll hear it for yourselves," she said. The recorded conversation Karen had with Leslie popped on the screen, and there she was, in rare form. Karen looked at Leila with a look so evil, but Leila just smiled.

Then Karen turned to Rayshon. "You knew all along, didn't you?" she barked at him, and he reached into his pocket and pulled out his wedding ring. He slid it on his finger and told Karen his true feelings about her.

"Yes, I knew, and you repulse me," he spat. Karen's eyes welled up with tears.

"I did it all for you," she cried.

"No, you did it all for you," he said, and then he turned to his wife. Leila stood on the stage with the biggest smile on her face.

"I love you," she cried, and Rayshon just nodded his head.

He turned back to Karen. "You are crazy, you know that, and for Shon's sake, you need to get some help. Now, stay the fuck away from my family and me," he bellowed and walked away.

"Looks like *I* got the last laugh," Leila chuckled and left the stage.

Karen watched Rayshon grab his wife by the hand while she descended the stage steps. She wanted to rip Leila's head off. The widest smile graced Leila's face as Rayshon pulled her into his arms and kissed her.

Karen was seething, and she stood there as her friends and family walked by her with looks of disgust. When her mother approached, Karen wanted to punch her too, because she'd bet she also was in on it. "You knew about this?" she asked.

"Of course, I didn't. Do you think I would have just left you to the wolves?"

"Please, you've never tried to protect me," she said.

"Yes, I have, and since I see nothing has changed, I'll be keeping Shon for a while," her mom declared and walked away.

Karen was mortified. She needed to get out of there. She walked out and remembered she didn't drive. "Fuck!" she said. And when she turned and saw Leslie exit the club, she charged her, and security instantly broke them up.

"How could you betray me?" she yelled.

Leslie eyed her. "Karen, you are crazy, and you got everything you deserved. I don't care if I lose my license because what I did was so wrong and wasn't worth hurting Rayshon and Leila. I advise you to stay the fuck away from me, and if you ever run up on me like that again, I'm going to whip your ass," she said for the first time standing up to Karen. "I'm not afraid of your crazy ass anymore." She picked up her purse from the ground and walked away. Karen stood there, breathing hard, thinking she was going to get her ass too after she got Leila. Then she hailed a cab and rode home with revenge on her mind.

Meanwhile, back inside . . .

"We did it, baby," Leila said, and they kissed.

"You were amazing," Rayshon said, and they continued to sway to the music.

"I can't wait to get home."

He grabbed her hand. "I can't either," he said with a smile. They went over to Kennedy to let her know they were leaving and thanked her and Julian for helping with their master plan. They told Kennedy they'd come back to pick up their laptop and tape later. When they got home, they sent Tabitha home and made crazy love.

Chapter Forty-four

When Karen got home, she was not happy to see her mother's car parked in front of her building. She climbed the stairs wondering why she just didn't go home. When she walked into her place, her momma was sitting on the sofa, smoking a cigarette. The sight of Karen made her shake her head.

"Ma, why are you here?"

"Because I need to talk to you, and I have a barrel of questions running through my mind. I don't know why you turned out this way. I don't know where I went wrong with you."

"Yeah, you don't know why, right?"

"No, I don't, Karen, I honestly don't. This is the fourth time, baby. The last time this happened, I thought you were over it. I thought you got help, but I see you live to destroy lives," her mom said. "You always fall for the wrong man. You still manage to go after someone that you know you can't have. You were 15, Karen, when you had your first affair with Mr. Milton, a married man. That man lost everything behind you and all the damage you did, stalking him and harassing his wife. You drove him out of the state to get away from you.

"Then senior year, Mr. Yates, and then college. Episode three when you got kicked out for sleeping with Professor Cannon, another married man. You act as if you can't see that what you are doing is wrong. And now, Ray. Karen, you are like poison, baby, and I want to help you. You need help," she said, and Karen just stood there as if she were lost in space.

"Oh, so I need help? Now, you are saying I need help? Why didn't you get me help after you found out your damn husband was raping me every damn night when you were working nights at Mercy?" she cried. Her mom's mouth opened, but no words came out.

"Come on, Mother, let's just be real while you're trying to get inside of my head and tell me I need help. Your nasty-ass husband thought it was okay to fuck me every time you were gone—a married man with a wife, who wasn't satisfied with the woman he had. Instead of his dirty ass going out in the streets to find a mistress, he made *me* his mistress, Momma. I was 13 when that pig started touching me. I begged you not to work at night, Momma, but you left me there with him!" she yelled.

"Karen, you know I didn't know, and you never said a word, Karen, and as soon as I found out, I put his ass behind bars. We went and sought help, Karen, and I did all I knew how. I asked you over and over and over again if you were okay, and you always said yes. You know damn well that I didn't *let* him hurt you, baby. Where I went wrong, Karen, was not making sure you were really okay. I want to help you now, but you gotta be willing, Karen. You are a grown woman, and you have to want to get help."

"You know what, Mother? You don't have to fight me for custody of Shon because I need a moment, okay? My life is gone to shit, and I can't deal with him right now anyway," she said. She went into the kitchen to pour herself a drink, and her mom came in.

"Karen, I'm worried about you, baby. Please talk to someone. Get some help. I'll go with you every day, Karen," her mother said, but Karen wasn't trying to hear her.

"Mother, I'm fine. I'm not crazy, and I don't need help. You can pick Shon's things up tomorrow, and whatever papers you need to draw up, get them, and I'll sign them," she said, then took a swallow of her drink.

"Karen, baby, what are you planning to do? Are you going to get some help, baby? You really should talk to someone," she pleaded, but Karen didn't want to hear her.

"Good night, Mother," she said, then walked past her and went into her room and slammed the door. She sat on the bed and finished her drink while thoughts of getting into her car and going over to Rayshon's house and killing them both played in her head. "It's okay, Karen, you're going to be okay," she told herself out loud. "You are going to be just fine, and you're going to pay them back for what they did to you," she said, and her eyes burned. She waited to hear the front door close before she opened her bedroom door.

Chapter Forty-five

What went down at the club was the talk of the town. Karen quit South Suburban because she couldn't show her face. Her mom did what she said she would do to get custody of her baby, and Karen didn't fight her because she needed to be alone. Besides, she was in no shape to care for him, so she signed him over without any dispute.

After two months of crying and feeling sorry for herself, she decided she was ready to go through with it. She was going to kill Leila. That was the only way she could make Ray feel some of her pain. Leila was his everything, and she wasn't going to rest until she got revenge. For a month, she'd sit outside and watch her house and her routine so that she could catch Leila off guard. She was ready that morning when she sat and watched Leila put her kids on the school bus. After she watched Rayshon leave for work, she got out. She approached the house slowly, opened the gate, and went into their backyard.

She walked over to the back door, turned the knob, and was happy to find the door was unlocked. The sound of the door chime was unexpected, but she crept inside anyway to find their first floor empty. Karen walked around and checked out their home. She gripped the knife handle tighter when she examined their family photos. She stood still when she heard Leila's voice singing to the baby. Soon, Leila walked into the kitchen, holding little Rayven—and froze when she saw Karen standing in her family room.

"Oh my God, Karen," she said, startled. "What are you doing in my house?" she yelled, trembling with her daughter in her arms.

"What do you think I'm doing here?" Karen asked with a crazy look in her eyes. "I'm here to make you pay for what you did to me, bitch," she barked.

"Karen, whatever you came to do has nothing to do with my baby. Please don't touch my baby," Leila cried.

"What, you think I would hurt your baby?" she said like she wasn't crazy. "Put her down," she instructed, and Leila moved slowly over to Rayven's playpen. She put her down, then stood and eyed Karen.

"Okay, Karen, why are you here in my home?"

"Why am I here?" Karen laughed. "Why am I here? I'm here because the life you are living is the life *I'm* supposed to be living. Get your ass over here and sit down," she yelled, and Leila did.

"Let me take you back to the night I met Rayshon. He was tall, fine, and the most decent brother that I had ever met. After he fucked me right, he got up and made me breakfast the next morning and treated me like I was a queen. He did things to my body that no man had ever done, and just that one night I spent with him, I fell for him.

"Do you know he strung me along and lied to me, Leila, making me think that he was interested, and then I find out the reason he stops taking my calls was because of you. If he knew I didn't have a chance and he was interested in you, he should have never hooked up with me. He should have never done that to me," she said, crying.

"Karen, I understand how you must have felt, but that was so long ago, and I'm sure Ray never meant to hurt you," she said.

"But he did!" she yelled, and Leila jumped. "And killing you will be the only way I can hurt him the way he hurt me," she said, and tears formed in Leila's eyes.

"Please, Karen, you don't want to do this. Killing me won't take away your pain."

"Shut up, bitch. You don't know me, okay? You can't figure me out, bitch, so don't try," she yelled and pulled out the knife. It was a surgical instrument, and Leila looked terrified.

"Please, Karen, don't do this. Not in front of my baby," Leila begged, and Karen looked at Rayven in her playpen playing with her toys.

"Get up," Karen demanded, and Leila did what she said. "Get Rayven and let's go upstairs," she said. Leila got her baby from her playpen and was shaking like a leaf. Karen walked close to her with the blade and followed her to Rayven's nursery, where Leila put her down. "Where's your bedroom?" Karen asked, and Leila pointed. She shoved her toward her room, and Leila walked slowly.

"Look at this shit," Karen said. "This is going to be *my* bedroom when I'm done with you," she stated and made Leila sit on the chaise. She was standing over her when they heard the door chime, and a female's voice called out Leila's name. Karen jumped, and Leila charged her. They began to roll around on the floor.

Leila used all of her strength to keep Karen from stabbing her, but the blade sliced her shoulder, and Leila screamed in pain.

"Leila!" she heard Tabitha's voice again, and she knew she had come upstairs.

"Tab, get Rayven and get out of the house and call the police," Leila yelled.

Leila struggled on the floor, trying to get Karen off of her. She pushed as hard as she could and finally succeeded. She tried to scramble for the door, but Karen was on her again, and the blade caught Leila's calf. She screamed again and kicked Karen in the face with all of her might, trying to get to her gun. Karen fell backward.

Leila scrambled to her feet with blood dripping from her shoulder and leg, and it stung like hell. Karen was up on her feet and blocked the door and the path to Leila's gun.

"I'm going to kill you, bitch!" Karen yelled and charged at Leila again and tried to slash her face, but Leila grabbed her hand. Karen struggled to break free, but Leila wouldn't let go, so she punched her in the face with her other fist. Leila fell back and hit her head on the tile of the fireplace. Karen came at her again, but Leila grabbed a log from the pile and hit her across the head. Karen fell back. The knife flew across the room. Leila went for Karen and hit her again and again, till she didn't move, and then she dropped the log and began to cry. A few moments later, the police rushed in. Leila was sitting close to Karen's body with the log near her hand. The police demanded that she put her hands up, and she did.

She was shaking and crying as the police came over and checked Karen's pulse. She was still alive. Another officer came over to Leila to check her wounds. The paramedics showed up and took both of them to the hospital. Leila was trembling. She wished she would have killed Karen's crazy ass.

After Leila got twelve stitches in her shoulder and seven stitches in her calf, two officers questioned her.

When they got home, and Ray saw all the blood in their bedroom, he decided they would sleep in the guest room until they replaced the carpets and cleaned the traces of Leila's injuries from their room.

Karen was arrested and was charged with attempted murder, trespassing, breaking and entering, intent to harm with a deadly weapon, and any other charge they could throw at her. She made a plea of insanity and was committed to a psychiatric facility for an indeterminate period. At the final sentencing, she sat there with a blank stare in her eyes as her mother sobbed through the entire ordeal.

She lost custody of her son to her mother, and when they left the courthouse, Karen's mom approached Leila and Rayshon.

"Listen, Rayshon, I am deeply sorry for everything. The day I met you in the hospital, I wanted to warn you that Karen had issues after I found out you were married, but I believed that she had gotten help and that she was better. I am so sorry, and although I hate to say these words, my daughter needs to stay locked away for a long time for what she has done to you and your family," she said. Rayshon and Leila accepted her apology and knew she was not to blame for Karen's attempt on Leila's life.

"Mrs. Morgan, it's okay. Rayshon and I will be fine. We have each other, and we will be okay," Leila said.

"Yes, Katherine, we'll be fine. If ever you need help with Shon, please, you have my number. Don't hesitate to ask. I know I can't be in his life physically anymore, but I love him, and I know that none of this is his fault, so please know that we will be here for him," Rayshon said squeezing Leila's hand, and as bad as everything was, Leila didn't disagree. She knew Shon was just as much a victim as she was, so she was proud of Rayshon for offering to be there for the baby.

Karen was taken to a holding cell until she was scheduled to be taken away. She sat there emotionless and still didn't see that she was the unstable one in the entire scenario. She spent every day of her sentence planning how she could kill Leila if she ever got out.

The End